Flotilla: M

By Eri

Self publishing

P.O. Box 523

Nine Mile Falls, WA 99026

Cover Photo © 2016 PathDoc / ShutterStock.com license

Manufactured in the United States of America

FIRST EDITION

ISBN 978-1539654971

For Karen. You will be missed.

Prologue

I tapped my toe like an impatient mother on the heavy timbers of the dock at the Flotilla Project. I muttered to my companions as I checked the time on my mobile, "Where is that woman, we have to go sign the paperwork on the property today?"

Angie just had a smug look on her face. I pointed at the tall woman and squinted my eyes at her in mock warning. "I know she'll make it. Don't presume you know Tabby better than me. She's been my best friend for better than half my life now so I've the latitude to whine. Do I need to remind you of the proper response?"

I tried so very hard not to chuckle. Our new runner, Lenore, well I guess I can't call her new anymore since she has been with us for eighteen months, droned out cutely as if she were reciting a lesson. "The two proper responses are 'yes ma'am' or 'yes Paya.'"

She gave us both a toothy grin and Angie grabbed her face and gave a playful shove. "Stop sucking up Speedy, it will only make the Indian-Brit's head swell bigger. Then she won't be able to get it through doors and such, it'd be a terrible inconvenience."

My laughter bubbled up and out of me like it came from some babbling brook deep inside. I loved my employees. They were more friends, nay, family to me than workers. I squinted an eye at Speedy. She had come a long way since the day Angie brought her home with her like a lost puppy.

She found her on the streets, not even eighteen yet, half starved and too many servings of pride within her to accept help. Bloody hell, was she really about to turn nineteen next month? She reminded me so much of Angie herself when I took her under my wing, when she was in a similar situation.

I could all but hear the question in her voice when she introduced her to me, when she hired her for a day to help us move one of the people in our Slingshot program, into their new flat. "Look what I found? Can we keep her?"

Just looking at the girl made my heart ache in memory. She reminded me so much of my best friend ever, Tabitha Romanov, when she was on the streets herself, living in the floating slums, the rickety makeshift dwellings on the rundown barges. Back when she was a water gypsy and I didn't have the means to help her the way she deserved, even though she was too proud to ever accept it anyway.

Lenore looked simply starved, like Tabby, before her insane musical talent was discovered by London Harmony. I think in some ways I'll be forever scarred from seeing my friend in that situation and feeling so helpless, not being able to help.

I watched as Angie used the same method I had used on her to help her to find her own self-worth again, by giving her honest work and a roof over her head. One side job became two then three, then more. Before long she was pretty much our permanent runner, and she was fast. So much so our friend, June, had branded her with the Speedy nickname and it stuck.

In the first few weeks, she stayed with Ange in the Captain's quarters in the Persephone. Since of course, it only made sense to keep her close to save time from driving to pick her up for work each day. That it gave the girl a roof over her head was a happy coincidence, right?

Then the woman who holds the entirety of Angie's heart, Stephanie Draper, thought the arrangement silly and asked Angie to move in with her and her children. Angie agreed in an instant. She would move heaven and earth for Steph and her children.

Now Speedy is the sole occupant of that cabin up in the pilot house of the modernized barge. She has grown to have pride in herself again, and having a place she can call her own has helped immensely.

I can't help but feel like she's my own little sister, and I know Ange feels the same.

I looked at her through my squinted eyes and squished my lips to one side of my face as I asked, “You remembered to eat breakfast this morning didn't you, Speedy? You look positively starved.”

Ok so maybe she didn't look starved, but I have this weird panicky feeling all the time after seeing Tabby get light headed and passing out once when she forgot to eat back then.

Speedy rolled her eyes and sounded every inch a teenager as she said in an exasperated tone, “Bloody hell. Yes 'mum,' I ate breakfast. Mostly to keep you from asking.” Her exasperation turned into a grin as she pulled her unnaturally curly brown hair out of her face and twisted it into a ponytail, sliding the orange scrunchy from her wrist onto the unmanageable nest. "And we can all see how that worked out for me."

I gave her a half smirk. "Cheeky today are we?"

The clunky old sedan that pulled into the car park of the Flotilla saved her from a witty retort from your's truly. I shook my head as a smiling copper haired rockstar stepped out and waved at all of us. I kept shaking my head and smiled back as we all stepped off the dock and past the rustic benches that gave a spectacular view of the Thames and the London skyline.

The woman was worth millions, and if she stopped singing today, the residuals from her Tabby Cat hits would support her nicely for the rest of her life, and a few more lifetimes. Cats had nine after all didn't they? She could have afforded any vehicle or fleet of vehicles she wanted, yet she insisted on the old Hillman Imp.

It was the kind of car her father drove when she was just a little girl, so she feels safe with it. She has never felt really comfortable with her newfound wealth and often shares that she feels like an imposter in someone else's life. The only thing she has bought for herself was the Water Witch. A spectacular houseboat she has harbored here on the Thames just downstream from her baby, the Flotilla Project. She says she fell in love with the waterways and couldn't imagine living on the land again.

Most of the rest of her money goes into the Flotilla Project and its associated programs. She partnered with the prior owner of the rundown barges the water gypsies like her lived on. The floating slums she used to call home.

The manky bint decided to punish me for loving her and not giving up on her when she was at her lowest, by making me an equal partner, and put the reins for managing the foundation in my hands. Fine, I love the silly bird, now shush, I'm telling a story here.

The barges were retrofitted and renovated into spectacular multi-unit condos that the project either lets out to people who have fallen on hard times, or provides the rooms for free. All in an attempt to put a roof over their heads until they can get themselves back on their feet again.

Sadly, the demand for rooms on the barges is overwhelming. There are so many people that go unseen by most, the destitute, the people who have fallen on hard times which have almost broken them in more ways than one.

It physically hurts me inside that we can't do more. It truly ties my insides up in knots at times so much that I find it difficult to breathe. But I put on my smile like armor, and soldier on. We keep finding new ways to expand the help we can provide with various programs, like the Slingshot Program.

We partner with dozens of property owners of muti-family dwellings all across London. They provide heavily discounted leases for the people in the program when they are ready to move out of the barges and into a place of their own when they can financially afford to.

The participants pay a flat rate of two hundred and fifty quid a month, which included utilities and a private bath. Our foundation pays the rest to the landlords. As long as the residents live in the units provided, the rate would never change, making it affordable for anyone on low or fixed income to have their own place, and regain their own self-worth.

The sad part of the whole thing, is the sick joke that it still isn't enough. There are more people out there needing our help than we can place with the participating properties. The waiting list for the people on the Slingshot list has grown from one month to almost six months before we can find them a place they can hang their hats.

The new barge, the Jabberwocky, which arrived just two months back to join the other five in the Flotilla fleet, is already full up.

We were at one of the traditional Thursday Night gatherings on the Water Witch six months back. Tabby and I were talking to June and the others about how there just weren't enough flats available to the Project. We weren't even able to tread water anymore as we fell further and further behind while we tried to sign other properties.

June had just shrugged and asked, "So why wait for properties to open up then?"

I had squinted an eye at her and said, "Don't be cryptic you bloody Yank. You have that 'it's so simple' look on your face. Don't make me drag it out of you."

She said in her singsong voice as her toddler, Emily, squirmed on her hip, “Yes Paya.”

I gave her a toothy grin. “There's a girl.”

She looked between Tabitha and I and asked like it was the simplest thing in the world, “Why wait for properties to open up, why not use some of the Flotilla funds to purchase your own properties or build?”

Ok, sometimes I hate loving that woman. June says things like that like they are simple, and she's right. We get our blinders on looking at one solution that we forget there is a slew of other possibilities. Tabs turned her copper eyes on me and looked as sheepish as I felt and she asked, “Can we do that?”

My playful glare at June, which got the wicked woman laughing heartily at us, was my answer. I countered her with, “I still dress better than you.” Then I raised my chin imperiously before my chuckle escaped.

She was right, and it was something we had never considered. We quickly found out why. In the London core, there was a serious lack of available buildings. Let alone apartment blocks. If we needed a warehouse, you couldn't throw a stone down by the old docks without hitting one.

But to find what we needed, we had to go to the outskirts of the city, and we wanted to service the core first, where most of the homeless community congregates. People feel more comfortable in familiar surroundings, and relocating them to unfamiliar suburbia would be a jarring adjustment.

June came to our rescue, again. It seemed there was a man who owed her a favor, and he had an old vacant rental property by the Hammersmith. An apartment block just a street removed from the Thames, the Steinberg. He had run out of funds when he was modernizing and retrofitting the twelve units in the rustic building to bring them up to code when the economy tanked.

He was more than happy to deal with us to get the 'money pit', as he called it, out of his portfolio. It has been a nightmare with the city and the borough council to finalize the sale, and to make sure any work we did on the building preserved its historic integrity.

Today, we finally sign the papers and the Steinberg is ours. We are meeting with the seller, the bank, and the superintendent we are hiring to manage the building, Mrs. Smythe. She manages many of the properties the Slingshot Program works with, and I find her perfect to be the matron of our first building.

If this works out, we may pursue other properties. But that is a while off, there is a lot of work left to do before we can open the doors of the Steinberg to our residents.

Anyway, I digress. Tabs has her arms open for a hug, so who am I to deny her? I hugged my best friend. "Hey, brat."

She responded with her familiar, "Hiya Paya."

I grinned then looked at the women. "Right then, shall we be about it?"

They nodded in assent and we all started walking toward my SUV, except Tabs, who started back to her rickety automobile.

She looked over at us then changed course and hustled to keep up, she whined out, “Hey you bints. What's wrong with my vehicle?”

Ange didn't miss a beat as she replied with a crooked half smile, “You really want the entire list, or just the obvious?”

Tabitha clamped her mouth shut, she could sling sarcasm around like confetti, so I knew she was restraining a smart arse comment through her grin as her eyes sparkled with mischief.

We reached my SUV and Speedy offered, “I'll drive.”

As one we all swung to her, our eyes wide and snapped out in unison, “No!” Trust me, there's a reason.

We all chuckled at her pouty look and saddled up. I admit that I was buzzing with excitement.

Chapter 1 – The Steinberg

"Aww man," I whined as I followed Paya and the others to the foundation's oversize SUV. They never let me drive. I'm not that bad. Well kinda, but still, aww man.

Angie thought I'd be more versatile and useful for the Flotilla if I got my license. Let's face it, running around doing errands for the group on public transit is not the most efficient way to do things.

So when Ange said, "We're going to have to teach you to drive, Speedy," I didn't even balk at the nickname since I was pretty excited about the prospect. I had always wanted to drive.

After two lessons and much yelling later, she was pale as a ghost as she handed me off to Paya. Bloody hell is Paya dreamy, and she always looks so posh, without a hair out of place. But after just a few minutes in the passenger seat, she muttered, "Oh hell no." That's how I wound up enrolled in a driving school.

Six weeks later I had my bright and shiny new license, thank you very much. I ignore the suggestions from my evil bosses that they simply passed me in the class just to preserve their nerves and heart health.

They make me drive the Flotilla's supply truck instead of these sleek SUVs which the rest of them get to drive, but I don't complain much since hey, I get to drive!

I slid into the back seat with Angie, because as we have all been informed by Paya, Tabitha has the shotgun position in perpetuity. Just how surrealistic is it that I know Tabby Cat? I mean, I grew up listening to her music.

I admit to feeling like a 'kid,' always being relegated to the back seat, and I guess I shouldn't complain since I've really only been an adult for just a year now. Though it feels like so much longer. The nine months I spent on the streets felt like decades to me. Maybe there is some sort of time dilation effect that occurs when we find ourselves at our lowest?

They all treat me like their kid sister, and I must admit that I sort of love it. I mean, to have people actually care about you and give you genuine smiles when they see you? I'll take the back seat all day every day for the warmth that causes inside me each time. It feels like family is supposed to feel. You are supposed to be happy whenever you see family, instead of scared or ashamed.

I just sat back with a perma-grin on my face as we started down the lane and Tabby started singing, the other girls joined in. Pays didn't have the perfect pitch that Tabby had, but she was no slouch herself.

Angie was a whole other thing, besides being Paya's right-hand woman and girl Friday, she also sang backup for Tabby on her albums. It was amazing to hear them singing together in person, and I always felt so privileged to witness it in person so often.

Tabs kept looking back at me, wiggling her eyebrows in a prompt to join in. Ange bumped my shoulder. “Come on Lenny, you know you want to.”

I explained as the other two continued singing, unimpeded by our conversation, "I sound like a bull walrus being mauled by a colony of rabid platypus and you know it, Boss."

Tabby let out an explosive giggle before recovering and continuing to sing. I pushed my ponytail back over my shoulder. I hated my hair, it had a life of its own, and after almost nineteen years I still haven't figure out how to tame it.

Angie sighed heavily. "You know it doesn't matter, it's all about having fun and letting loose. You don't have to act like an old retired spinster all the time, lady. And stop calling me Boss."

I shot her a sly smile. "You got it, Boss." She'd be Boss until she stopped using June's evil nickname for me. Speedy isn't all that bad, all things considered, compared to the dreaded Lenny I keep getting stuck with, just like back in school. But as you can imagine, there aren't many things you can do with a name like Lenore.

I'm pretty sure my parents had it out for me from the very beginning as my middle name isn't much better, Guinivere. I tried going by Gwen for a while, but it didn't stick. I cringed whenever mum would three name me when I was in trouble. I can hear it now. "Lenore Guinevere Statham, honestly, what were you thinking?" Well, my last name isn't really Statham, but you get the idea.

Tabs was now bouncing in her seat, prompting me with the words of the song. I had always thought when I saw her posters and music videos that she had to be wearing color contacts or that the images were all digitally edited. So imagine my surprise when I found out that her oddly copper colored eyes which matched her copper colored hair were natural. That just made her even more unique to me.

I blushed and looked down at my hands and croaked out the lyrics to 'Water Gypsy' with the group. They seemed genuinely pleased with me butchering the tune. I relaxed my inhibitions and belted out the words with the rest.

We were all laughing at the end of our third song when we pulled into the Hammersmith district. We crossed below the bridge on Lower Mall, paralleling the Thames. It truly was a gorgeous old bridge. Tower Bridge gets plastered all over the press, tourist fliers, and postcards, while other architectural classics like this get pushed to the wayside.

I noted it was low tide, and even this far inland, with the Thames being a tidal river, the brackish water level can have a two or three-meter change. There were a couple pleasure boats and fishing craft sitting on the sandy loam of the riverbank, just waiting for high tide to come free them again. That can't be good for the boat hulls, can it? But for as long as I can remember, I have seen this all up and down the Thames since I came to London.

I noticed one boat was painted a bright green. It looked like an old barge, but it had stacks of lumber, old doors, and windows all over its main deck. A banner was stretched across the railing that read, "McGrath Handyman Service" I had to grin. That was different, a workabout situated on a boat rather than in a proper workshop.

We turned north and went up one lane and pulled up to an apartment block that had some scaffolding and plastic covering some of the exterior like it had been abandoned mid-job. This wasn't the Steinberg, was it? It was a dump. It had potential, with the dark brickwork from the late 1800's and historic feel to the architectural features which you just don't see in modern buildings. But it looked to be in sad disrepair. Like the fact that half the windows were out of the building with tattered plastic covering the holes.

I had been excited to see the place since the girls had found it, they raved about it almost every day as they fought the city when the building council tried to block the sale. They viewed the people from the Flotilla to be... unsavory. The borough thought that it would negatively impact their district having a 'charity' building in their midst.

But Paya is great at making waves, it's what she does. She knows so many people, like June from London Harmony who threatened to pull some of their events which generate revenue for the city, if they blocked the sale. Funny thing that, the city pushed it through.

The girls sounded like a bunch of squealing teenagers when it was approved. So here we are today to make it all real.

I glanced at the building again then shook my head. The council complained about unsavory, yet they let the place look like a dump in their borough? Didn't that have a negative impact on the area? I swear I'll never figure people out.

We piled out of the vehicle and stared up at the ailing structure. There were the common patches of lighter bricks visible from repairs after the Blitz. And I had to admit that the stylish stonework on the parapets with the great sweeping stone angel wings which were chained along the length of the building, were pretty cool. There was a stone wreath of feathers above the entrance Why didn't they do artistic, architectural features like that on buildings anymore?

I could appreciate the building for what it had once been in a bygone era, but not to the extent that the girls were looking at it like forlorn, lost loves. I mean, I get it, I really do. It comes down to seeing the possibilities, not for themselves, but for the people we can help get back on their feet with the potential the building had.

At that realization, I looked at them and then it really clicked. These ladies had saved me from myself when I was at a point I didn't think I could drop any lower. I was begging on the street corner for lolly to eat, for God's sake. This was another way they could save others. I swear by all that is holy that one day I'll make them proud of me and I'll do the same thing for others. Pay it forward.

Another woman was striding down the walk with purpose as she looked at her watch. I grinned at the middle aged, slightly plump woman who had the mannerisms of a strict school matron.

She, as always, was in a smart business suit, a satchel slung over her shoulder.

Mrs. Smythe managed multiple tenancy buildings in core. She was strict, precise, and damn good at her job. She shows a cold, no-nonsense front, but I have her number.

I'm always standing back from the group, fading into the woodwork, a bad habit I got into on the streets. People ignored me, and I sort of got used to it. My new pseudo-family always gets upset when one of them sees me doing it around them. I don't really mean to, but it comes in handy at times, to separate myself from a situation and look in at it from a different perspective.

And I am always catching Mrs. Smythe smiling at how happy the girls are when they place another resident from the Flotilla into their own flat. And especially around Stephanie's children, Wil and Natalie, when they are hanging around with Angie when Steph needs a sitter. The woman is a soft touch, and she doesn't want anyone to see it.

I did what I always do around her just to rub it in, I saluted as she stepped up to us as we arrived at the front doors of the building. The woman schooled her face, though the corner of her mouth was twitching as she said, “Miss Doshi, punctual as always.” Then she turned to the rest of us and acknowledged us. “Mrs. Romanov, Miss Wells.” She couldn't stop the quirk of a smile as she added toward me. “Unruly child.”

I grinned and said tongue in cheek, “Nice suit, did you get it pressed at..." I trailed off when Paya arched an eyebrow at me expectantly, and Ange slapped the back of my head lightly. I cut short my retort then grinned and said like a schoolgirl reciting lessons, "It's good to see you, Mrs. Smythe."

Angie offered to the woman, who was trying so hard not to smile, "See? She can be taught." Then after a beat added, "Sort of." I reached up and returned the slap to the back of her head. Then stepped forward quickly before I could suffer any other playful ribbing, and held open the door for the others and prompted, "Ladies."

They smirked and headed through the twin dark, heavy hardwood doors which had huge almost floor to ceiling leaded glass pane inset into it. The glass had those same angel wings etched into it at the top, and a wreath etched into the center. The ghost-like white etchings looked almost like spirits floating across the smoky glass surface. Ok, now that was pretty cool. I was starting to like the place... then I turned to look inside.

Nope.

The lobby was a mess of construction material, tarps and plastic draped all over the floor and walls. There were holes in the walls down the length of them, exposing wiring and beams. What a dump. I couldn't tell if the place was being demoed for the renovation or if it were damage from vandalism that happened over the years as the structure sat vacant. I was doubly amazed now that the glass in the main doors had miraculously remained intact.

The ladies looked around with smiles of wonder on their faces that just forced a grin out of me. Mrs. Smythe's face was still carefully schooled as she followed Paya. I stepped over a stack of old wood that had toppled to block part of the entryway. Then our erstwhile leader did what she did and led us... down the corridor and through a doorway near the back, which had plastic sheeting hanging down over the opening.

There were three men in the room that looked like an office space you would expect in a schoolhouse. There was a counter and an open office beyond with a door leading into what looked like a private office.

I looked at the men as Paya stepped confidently up to the best dressed of the lot. He was a stout bloke in a smart suit complete with black tie. I didn't even need to guess, he had to be the banker.

The second man I knew well, Mr. Phennington, the official council for both the Flotilla Project and as it so happened, the London Harmony record label.

As far as solicitors went, Mr. P was a stand-up bloke. More relaxed than most stick-up-the-ass, charge by the second shysters out there. His trousers and white polo shirt attesting to that. The trim middle-aged Welshman preferred that attire to the stuffy suits those of his profession generally favored.

He was running his fingers through his frosted, mousy brown hair when we stepped in. He looked up and smiled at us as we filed into the space and looked around.

The third man was quite tall, and dressed casually, his bald black head and his rimless glasses gave him a sort of regal look. His smile was all it took for me to know he was immensely relieved to see us. Did he think Paya was going to back out on the deal? I glanced back the way we came. Yeaaahhh... ok, I get it. I'd be anxious to dump the dump myself.

He was the first to step forward from where the men had been looking over some old blueprints and a stack of papers on the room's dividing counter.

He held out his large hand to Paya, and I noted the sparkling Rolex on his wrist. Wow. Real estate acquisition must be a lucrative pursuit. “Miss Doshi, I'm glad you could make it.” She took his hand, and he cupped his other hand over hers. The way his large hands encased her delicate hand, made hers look like a child's toy.

She was nothing but toothy smiles as she shook in earnest, “Paya, please Gordon. And I wouldn't have missed this for the world.”

His smile changed to shock as he glanced over to us. He blinked at Tabitha, then realized he had been shaking Paya's hand for far too long while in shock over seeing a rock superstar in our midst.

Our Indian-Brit rolled her eyes, her smile not faltering as she said, “Gordon, the creator of the Flotilla Project, and my personal best friend, Tabitha Romanov. Tabby, this is Gordon Leavens, the soon to be ex-owner of this fine building.”

Tabs stepped forward with a little smirk at the star struck man and offered a hand. "Pleased to meet you finally, Paya has kept me in the loop during the negotiations Mr. Leavens."

He shook enthusiastically, sputtering out, "Gordon, please."

She nodded and said, "Gordon then." Then she offered, "Tabs." Then she looked at their shaking hands and the man a couple times before snorting when he realized they were still shaking. He released her hand looking a little sheepish as he ran a finger inside his collar nervously.

The banker, Mr. Herbert was introduced next, then Paya offered to everyone, "And these ladies here are our my executive assistant and Master of the Persephone, Angie Wells. And our Jill of all trades, and foundation runner, Lenore Statham." We exchanged nods with the men, and they got down to business.

They sifted through the mountain of paperwork, Phennington explaining a few things about restrictions on land use and caveats that the sale and any site improvements have to be vetted through the borough council and the Office of Historic Preservation.

They signed and initialed everything, Ange and I signing as witnesses. Then it was like we all exhaled a communal breath as Phennington and Herbert closed their folders and everyone straightened.

Gordon held up a ring of keys and offered it toward our leaders, he looked at them with hesitation, moving the keys between them and asking, "Tabs? Paya?"

Tabby almost giggled when Paya's hand shot out and snagged

the keys from the man. The crooked half smirk she shot Tabby was priceless as she said, "Oh shush you."

Tabitha chimed out like a schoolgirl as she fluttered her eyelashes innocently, "Yes Paya."

Our posh commander lifted her chin and looked down her nose at her best friend, "There's a good girl."

They exchanged toothy grins then looked up at the overly amused man towering over them. He chuckled and offered his hand to each and said as they shook, "Congratulations," We said our goodbyes and watched the men file out, business concluded.

Once we were alone, Paya spread her arms wide and spun in place as she tilted her head up like she were able to see the sky from inside and said with a touch of wonder in her tone, "It's ours. Imagine all the good we can do for people here."

Tabitha cocked her head and looked at her friend with warmth and compassion as she said, "You never got this excited when the new barge joined the Flotilla."

Paya looked back down and offered a challenge with an arched eyebrow. "The barges are wondrous, but they are just the temporary steppingstones for the people we help. This..." She spread her hands wide palms up, indicating the building. "This is permanent. This is that step back out, to give them pride in themselves again, to give them a place they can call home for as long as they want it."

Tabby softened then shared a smile with her and looked around with fresh anticipation.

Ok, there are many reasons I love these women, but this... this was the epitome of their true selflessness. I can't do much compared to them, but know I can help. I aspired to rise up to meet their ideals. Hopefully one day they would be proud to know me.

Tabby's stomach gurgled, and I glanced at my mobile, where had the bloody time gone? It was already almost noon, had it really taken so long to sift the papers?

Paya was staring at Tabitha's stomach accusingly and said, "Right then, let's get you all fed. The day is just begun. We have to meet with the council and the representative from the OHP at two. We need to get things rolling here to get the building buttoned up before snowfall."

I nodded staunchly. Right. No moss grows under our feet. I followed the ladies back out to our waiting vehicle. I offered as our two leaders got into an impromptu shoving match as we walked. "I can drive."

They all shouted back in unison, in abject terror, "No!"

***

That afternoon was one of those mind numbing experiences in my life that seemed to never end. The meeting with the council and OHP representatives amounted to a walkthrough of the building, studying the blueprints then two hours of them telling us all the things we could not do with our own building.

The only bright spot was when Paya mentioned, "We want to keep this local and hire people from Hammersmith to do the work when possible. Community building and all. Is there a general contractor you can recommend to oversee the workers and subs?"

The balding, stuffy old man, Brent Hastings, from the Office of Historic Preservation, had replied in his Churchill-like, jowled drawl, "My office can provide a list of preferred contractors and subcontractors from the area."

Then he said almost as a demand, "Just stay away from the McGrath Handyman Service. We do not approve of that pretentious Irish layabout."

I almost sighed at that. The man knew not what he did when laying out demands to our Paya. She cocked an eyebrow, and I saw Tabby bite her own tongue at the recognition of that. Then our Miss Doshi said in a surprised tone that was worthy of a BAFTA, "Oh my. We have already contracted with McGrath, was that inappropriate?"

Ms. Jones from the borough council made a derisive sound and Hastings grunted disapproval and Tabitha said, tongue in cheek, "Thank you both for meeting with us. We'll call when we do the walkthrough with our contractors to make a punch-list of upgrades and restorations."

They didn't like being dismissed like that, but they said their goodbyes and we all walked to the window of the room we were in on the second floor and watched until they stepped outside to their vehicles.

Then Paya burst out into a giggle that was far too cute and said, "So. I have no clue who this McGrath is, but we need to hire him. If he can make the stuffy Wonder Twins there that flustered, then he'll be our point man on the project." She watched the cars pull into traffic and huffed as she shook her head incredulously, "Telling us who we can or can't hire."

Tabby chuckled. "Rein it in there slugger."

Paya stuck her tongue out at her then turned to us, "So first things first. We need to locate this McGrath then the fun can begin."

I remembered the green boat on the riverbank and said, "I know where they are located. I'll set up a meeting and the walkthrough."

We were agreed, and I was excited to meet this guy, anyone who could ruffle the feathers of the political types like that had to be someone I'd like to know. I mean, just how bad could this McGrath be?

Chapter 2 – McGrath

I growled out to Angie and Paya as I threw my jacket forcefully onto a chair in the pilot house of the Persephone, "Raaaaagh! I'm going to kill McGrath! You can't make me drive that sanctimonious ass around anymore. I love you two, but this is too much to ask!"

The manky bints looked over amused at my outburst.

I never knew there were actually people in this world I could hate with a purple passion, nor what it would feel like to have an actual arch nemesis. But McGrath was mine, and she was the most frustrating, belittling, aggravating individual that God had seen fit to punish mankind with.

What made matters worse was the fact that she was pretty fucking good at her job, so it would be exceptionally stupid to replace her with another general contractor for the renovation. I have been stuck being her personal taxi service for the project for the past three weeks and I swear I'm going to kill her and hide her body in the woods somewhere and sleep peacefully dreaming of rainbows and unicorns afterward.

Paya cocked her head in an overly cute manner and said, "She's not that bad Lenny." Then she looked at the time on her mobile and grinned. "And aren't you supposed to be doing a supply run with her in a few minutes?"

I glared at the women and then gave an exasperated, "Hraaagh," sound and grabbed my keys off the table and stomped out of the cabin as they burst into giggles. When they couldn't see me as I stomped down the outer stairs to the main deck, I smiled. They were too much fun to stay aggravated at. And it wasn't them I needed to vent my frustrations on.

I ignored the gangplank and just hopped over the side of the barge to land on the dock and then made my way to the flatbed supply truck beside the freestanding storage units for the residents on shore.

I hopped in, and in no time was roaring down the lane toward Hammersmith where the scourge of my existence was waiting. I thought back to that first day I contacted her using the number on the banner on the boat. I was pleasantly surprised that the owner was a woman. I guess I'm a bit guilty of stereotyping.

She sounded like a pleasant Irish woman on the call and agreed to do the walkthrough with us and then we could determine if she could help us, and what her rates would be for the project.

I coordinated with the council, and they said that Brent Hastings from the OHP would have point on the project. We scheduled the walkthrough for the next afternoon. We wanted to meet with McGrath a few minutes early to introduce ourselves and explain our objectives. Tabby wouldn't be joining us, leaving it to us to spearhead things. She had complete faith in Paya.

She met us right after lunch at the Steinberg, and I have to tell you, she was not at all what any of us expected.

We were all standing in the office looking at the old

blueprints again, while Paya absently sketched some ideas on a pad of paper. I was impressed, she had some artistic talent. We all looked to the doorway when someone lightly knocked on the doorjamb. “Hello? I was knocin' on the door but nobody came a runnin' so I let m'self in.”

We saw the shadow of the woman behind the plastic sheeting and Paya said, “Come on in. McGrath I assume?”

The woman said, “That'd be me.” Then she pulled aside the plastic and stepped through the doorway. I think my eyebrows may have been swallowed by my hairline in surprise.

The woman was perhaps six feet tall, and her muscles bulged and stretched the green tee she wore that had faded white lettering which read, McGrath Handyman Service, over a white shamrock.

She had heavy denim jeans on that showed signs of heavy wear and miscellaneous paint drips all over them. A tool belt hung down loosely off one hip laden with all manner of well-used tools, the heavy leather belt supporting it was buckled high on her other hip with a hammer hanging in a loop on it and a tape measure clipped to the belt.

Her heavy work boots completed the ensemble. There was no way of faking the look, it left me with no doubt that she was a hardcore, seasoned contractor.

The woman had a hard look on her face, which she seemed to go to extremes to avoid it looking too feminine. She failed. She didn't wear any makeup, and she had a certain hard sensuality. Her hair, so deep red it was bordering on black, was shaved on the sides and sported a pixie cut on what remained. It was a little spiky in areas where it was cut a bit too short.

The heavy freckles, which ran up her arms and wrapped teasingly around her bulging biceps, seemed to crawl out of her shirt collar and sprinkle her cheeks and nose.

She stared at us with intense hazel eyes, cataloging and categorizing. She moved right past me, ignoring me completely as she stepped up to Paya as she slipped off a work glove, tucking it in her belt, before offering her hand. “You must be Miss Doshi. You'd be bein' my boss if I take on yer little project here.” As they shook she said, “Name's McGrath and I'm very pleased to meetcha.”

Paya beamed up at her, I could see her wanting a better look at her hair but restraining herself from being obvious. “Paya, please. I'm glad you could make it on such short notice, but we are in a bit of a rush on this project. The city building commission is set to levy fees and fines if we don't get the renovation done in the next nine months.”

Then she asked as she dropped McGrath's hand, “What should I call you?”

The woman turned her body toward Angie, offering a hand, still looking at Paya as she said, “Just McGrath if ya please. Suits me better than mahy given name.” Then she turned to lock eyes with Ange as they shook.

Paya offered, “That is my executive assistant, Angie Wells. And over there...” She squinted cutely and stabbed a finger toward me, her hand right under her chin. "Is our runner, Lenore."

The woman said, "Angie." Then looked over her shoulder to regard me with a simply raised brow before apparently dismissing me as she turned back to my bosses. I bristled a little as I shifted on my feet. Alrighty then.

Then we spoke with her about what we were trying to accomplish. She listened attentively, nodding as she seemed to absorb it all, asking pertinent questions or interjecting ideas as we went.

When we were done, she absently shook her head. "While I'm an ambitious sort, this is a little beyond mahy usual scope of work. I'm just a handyman. I wouldn't be able to take on a job of this scope on mahy own and finish in the allotted timeframe. I'd be needin' to hire out subs fer the heatin' and plumbin', I can handle the electrical. You'd be better off hirin' a general contractor to coordinate it all instead of me. Much as this buildin' is a rare beauty." She winked at Paya. "Much like yerself, mind ya."

Paya gave her a cheesy grin. "Tell a girl no, then throw her a compliment?"

McGrath chuckled, and Paya shook her head. "I really like your ideas, and you seem to have a firm grasp on what we need. I wouldn't be opposed to you acting as general in this. We have the budget to do this right and a bunch of hands eager to help where they can. The future tenants of this building who are currently living on the barges in the Flotilla Project."

The redhead looked at us all, making a decision as she ran her ungloved hand through her hair, exhaled, then said, "Tell you what... first thing, don't be spendin' yer money all willy nilly, nor wavin' it about just because you can. Contractors will be seein' you as a mark for endless change orders. So let's do the walkthrough before decidin' anything. If I believe it's somethin' I can be doin' fer ya, then you'll have yerself a deal."

She handed over a wrinkled card she produced from her back pocket to Angie. "My hourly rate."

Ange blinked at the card then showed it to Paya who arched an eyebrow in surprise. "Ummm... I think this is an old card. You couldn't possibly work for this cheap."

The woman looked aggravated, and she shifted around and said, "Fine, you can be havin' the frizz-top here fetchin' mahy lunch for me then if you insist on wastin' lolly. If you have a problem with mahy rate, then I can be movin' on."

I bristled at her calling me frizz-top. I can't help it if my hair is so unruly. I haven't been able to tame the curls my whole life, that's why I keep it in a ponytail all the time. I sure as hell wasn't going to be fetching hers or anyone else's lunch. Well, except Paya's and Angie's... and if Tabby ever asked... and... oh just shut up.

The women exchanged looks as Ange handed the card to me. It had McGrath's contact information on it, the name Connor before the McGrath was crossed out with a pen. Then in bold type read 'Labor, ten pounds an hour.' That was barely a living wage. I looked at the card and her, and she raised an eyebrow in challenge at me and said, "Fetch us a fizzy or something before the suits show? I'm parched."

I narrowed my eyes at her. I was about to tear into her when Ange caught my attention. She had an apologetic look on her face as she nudged her chin toward the door with a pleading look on her face.

I exhaled and spun to the door, fine, just this once because the woman actually sounded competent and that's what we needed for the renovation, but never again.

I can't tell you how tempted I was to shake the can of cola when I returned from the little market a few buildings down the way. It was clear that McGrath didn't see me as anyone consequential. But I wasn't 'her' runner. I set the cola on the counter just beyond her reach when I returned and slid the tray with three piping hot coffees in front of the girls. We all greedily sipped as the Irish woman chuckled at my childishness and retrieved her cola.

She chugged the can then set it down and suppressed a burp, her cheeks bulging out like a pufferfish. Then we heard a man's voice calling out, "Miss Doshi?"

Paya called out, "In the office Mr. Hastings."

A few seconds later the man pulled aside the plastic sheet and poked his head in, saying in a satisfied tone, "A yes, here you are."

He was laden with a satchel which had some rolled up floorplans sticking out of it. He gave a sour look at McGrath who simply cocked an eyebrow at him. "Brent."

He bristled at her being so familiar and said in an acidic tone, "Miss McGrath." Then he looked around and brightened and offered his hand to everyone but McGrath. Ok, so maybe I liked the stuffy bloke, after all, he had the good taste to shun her.

Then he said as he dug in his satchel, "I don't mean to rush, but I have another meeting in just a bit. Mind if we get started?" He produced a tablet computer, and that signaled all of us to pull out our iPads.

I blinked at McGrath when she pulled out a ragged little notebook and a pencil from her toolbelt. Really? Isn't that like, you know, a little old school? Even Hastings was sort of modern, though his choice of tablets was baffling to me. Eh, old blokes, what ya gonna do?

I saw Angie cock an eyebrow ever so slightly at the handywoman as well. Paya grinned and opened her mouth to speak, but the Irish woman beat her to the punch. "Right then, shall we start from top to bottom?" Then she strode off like a woman on a mission. It had taken a two beat before we all started in motion after her when it became obvious she wasn't waiting for anyone.

She took the stairs in bounds and turned down a corridor to the end like she knew where she was going. We had to hustle to keep up with her. She pulled open a narrow door at the end which had a plastic sign on it that read, "Roof Access." Then she paused for us to catch up and held the door open for us to go through.

When everyone had passed through the door before me, I went to step through, and she released the door and moved swiftly up the stairs. I had to catch the door from closing and then ran up after them. I made an exasperated sound and pushed the rude woman from behind, causing her to stumble a little. I swear she chuckled. I know, I was being childish, but I swear she was trying to push my buttons for some unfathomable reason. Had I kicked her dog in a past life or something?

Paya held the door at the top, and we stepped out onto a tar roof. There were pipes and vents and semi-modern air conditioning units all over.

The one thing that caught my attention was a little wooden pergola just off the side of the door. There were a bunch of concrete pavers laid out across the tar roof to form a floor for the little structure, and there was a small outdoor bistro table with three little chairs in the middle of the space. Someone in the building's past life had used the roof as a getaway.

I studiously took notes as McGrath led the others around to examine the roof structure itself and look at the deterioration of the parapets. Hastings didn't have much input but to ask about restorative materials for the parapets, to make sure they wouldn't damage the historic angel wings on the facade. He explained that the roof wasn't really a concern for the OHP.

I admit I almost snorted when the Irishwoman said, "I'll be sure the mortar and concrete are made of sufficiently old rocks, like the ones you played with as a wee lad." Before he could comment she rolled her eyes, "Come on now Brent, it isn't as though they're carved stone. This was a budget building even back then."

Then she added with an odd wistful tone, "Though it did have promise."

The man huffed and headed back toward the door of the stairwell. He waved a hand at the pergola and said, "And get rid of this monstrosity."

Paya looked at the redhead who shrugged in apology. "A thin skin, that one." Then she graciously made an ushering motion. "Ladies. And Frizzy."

I shot her a death glare and her eyes twinkled in mirth. Ange came to my rescue. "Go easy on our Speedy here, would you?"

McGrath nodded and quickly responded, "Of course Miss Wells."

She made a show of holding the door for everyone including me this time. I swear she had a bloody smirk on her face when I passed by.

Then we looked at the corridor, McGrath said absently as she stared up at the cracked and damaged crown molding and laid a hand on the wall where some gaudy 1960's looking wallpaper was peeling. She said absently, "Right, we'll need to tear out that molding and replace it with something more period appropriate, it isn't worth restoring, especially with the time constraints." She looked at Hastings who looked ready to object and asked him, "Is the OHP going to be sticklers about period appropriate construction materials for wall construction?"

He blurted out, "Of course. The Steinberg may not hold much historical significance, but it is still on the historic register."

The woman sighed and seemed to deflate at that. "Right then, we'll have to be replacein' the wallboard in the corridors then. Maybe the flats as well once we have a look inside." She looked apologetically to Paya. "I'm tryin' to save ya lolly here, but the OHP is gonna be makin' this a spendy proposition with that single revelation ol' Brent just provided. I'm beginnin' to see why the original renovation was abandoned then with all the impediments, roadblocks, and the like."

Mr. Hastings puffed up. "Just see here young lady, the OHP is not impeding anything. It is our duty to ensure historical accuracy on any historic building renovations in London. That includes the Steinberg. You need to take every effort to restore that molding, it is original to the construction, and why are you inferring that the walls need to be demoed?"

She actually chuckled at the man and asked in a serious tone, "Are ye daft man?" She tucked her notepad into her tool belt, pulled her hammer from its loop, and stood on an overturned metal bucket near the wall.

Hastings almost squeaked in horror when she reached up and forcefully tore at a piece of the molding with the claw end of her hammer, widening the cracks until a chunk pulled free in a plume of dust when the wood snapped.

She stepped down and thrust the two-foot long chunk of wide crown molding in front of him and said simply, "Primroses and thistle, man."

He glared at her and said simply, "As on the royal coat of arms. Yes? I can't believe you just defaced a piece of history like a common vandal."

She huffed. "Brent. When was this buildin' constructed?"

He said matter of factly, "Eighteen eighty-nine."

She asked, "So in what year was our dear Queen brought into this world?"

He snapped out, "Nineteen twenty-six, everyone knows..." He trailed off, balked, and then stared at the molding in her hand with sheepish disbelief and understanding painting his face.

McGrath looked like the cat who swallowed the canary. "Yes, and she didn't take the throne until nineteen fifty-two, where something was added to the field of thistle on the Royal Arms." She had stated it as a prompt.

She stared at him expectantly, and he said grudgingly, "Primrose."

She gave him a toothy grin. The rest of us were lost until she explained to him, but I knew it was really for our education, "Precisely, this place is a contradiction. I've already seen evidence of two or three major renovations as we've moved along. Like the walls here. She swung her hammer so fast and hard I almost missed it. There was a thunking sound and the hammer smashed through the wall.

The man blustered again, but she held up her hand to him and grasped the wall through the hole and tore off a chunk and handed it to him. He cocked an eyebrow as his protest seemed to fizzle as he took the piece of wallboard.

She nodded to the man as she laid her hand and a cheek almost lovingly against the wall, saying, "That's right, sheetrock. Not the original lathe and plaster. You can feel it... the difference ya know."

She ran her hand along the wall then pulled back and locked eyes with him. "Sheetrock feels different. It has a warmth and hollowness, lackin' the mass and hardness of lath and plaster. And as you well know, sheetrock, Sackett Board, wasn't invented until almost a decade after this buildin' was constructed."

She explained to us what Hastings had realized earlier, "That, combined with this molding which commemorates the Queen's changes to the Royal Arms over a half century after this place was built, tells us that this renovation occurred most likely in the mid to late sixties seein' as how the electrics have grounds."

She looked almost accusingly at Hastings. "It was probably easier and faster for them to demo the wall coverin' to modernize the electrics and plumbing and throw up sheetrock than to endlessly cut and patch the plaster."

The man grudgingly nodded his assent to her argument, then pointed out as if in defense. "The building wasn't added to the historic register until the nineteen seventies, so we don't have much if any documentation on renovation projects before that. And the original documentation on the construction was lost in the Blitz so we only have the rough plans submitted to the city for a building permit. Being a residential structure, there aren't many photographs of the building, particularly the interior."

She shook her head and said almost in apology, "Come now Brent. I can be forgivin' ya the wallboard, you'd have no way of knowin', but the molding?"

His face just turned red in frustration. She looked back at us and winked as he said, "Ladies, shall we continue?"

Ok, now that was sort of hot how she tore apart the man who was supposed to know his history and about construction. We watched her do that time after time as we went through the building. I grudgingly admitted that the woman knew her stuff and was a surprising font of historical information. I just wished she wasn't such a sodding wanker.

We finally wound up in the main lobby after we did a quick perusal of the exterior. She brought us up to the end of the hall, past the stairs where a boxy protrusion came out from the rear wall. Then she prompted, "Will you be puttin' the old lift back in service or installin' a new one? Even the Office of Historic Preservation can't get around the accessibility codes."

Lift? Was that what was behind the wall? I saw Paya sigh. As the walk-through progressed, we could all see the costs multiplying exponentially. Now the cost of a lift. But it was a definite must. There was no way in hell the Flotilla would not have a building that wasn't accessible to those with disabilities.

She cocked her head at the toned workabout. “What would you suggest?”

The woman shrugged. “I know what Ol' Brent here wants, but restorin' an old lift could wind up costin' two or three times what a modern lift would. It all depends on its condition.”

She slipped her hammer from her belt again, and I squinted as she slammed it into the wall of the boxy protrusion. Hastings balked again and muttered, “Brash as your father.”

She paused, her hammer still buried in the wall and she turned slowly, there was no emotion at all on her face, and it sort of scared me as she spoke in a low, calm tone, “You'll not be desparigin' me Da, God rest his soul. Whatever problems you may have with me, you leave him out of it. Do I make myself clear... Brent?” Without any inflection of her tone, I felt as though there was a threat of extreme violence permeating the air suddenly. I swallowed.

Angie had her head cocked slightly, her eyes on the woman and I could see that she caught something that the rest of us may have missed about her because I saw her soften ever so slightly.

The redhead didn't blink, didn't move, and Hastings looked away first and said, “Of course. My apologies.”

Then she smiled and said with her Irish accent deepening to tweedledee as she slightly elongating the word with a third syllable and said, “Lovely.”

Then without looking at us, she proceeded to reach into the hole she had made and started yanking off large portions of wallboard. Chalk and dust mixing in the air as it gave way under her brutal assault. One chunk resisted and with a yank the entire section pulled away from the wall. She dragged it until it fell to the floor. She seemed to be working out whatever aggravation Hastings' comment had instigated with her demolition.

I could see a black cast iron cage in the space beyond. McGrath started slamming the hammer into the base of a joist until it gave way and she pulled and twisted, pulling the nails from their moorings above and she dropped the board on the floor with a clatter of wood on wood.

The opening was large enough to step through now, and she looked in, squinting, then reached behind a portion of the wall she hadn't torn apart like a human wrecking ball, and she moved something. The crisscrossed metal of the cage door seemed to relax, and she pulled it aside.

We all watched as she moved into the opening and released the inner cage and stood in the lift beyond. Paya stepped forward quickly, concern on her face. "Should you be in there? What if it falls?"

I looked reflexively at the floor. There cellar where the maintenance room was and the old coal chutes were down there. We were planning on putting in storage cages down there for the residents.

The woman poked her head back out the wall with a toothy

grin for our fearless leader. "This is an Otis Safety Elevator. It'd be neigh impossible for it to fall."

She popped back out of sight and said appreciatively, "Manual crank controls too. This is a rare beauty."

She stepped back out a moment later and gave an apologetic look to Paya. "Miss Doshi, that lift is a work of art. I'd be feelin' like we are doing her a disservice if we didn't restore her to her glory. She looks to be operational as she sits. I'd have to examine the lift cables and mechanism, but I don't see anything that would preclude a rapid return to service."

Angie asked, "You think it's operational? Why did they board it up?"

The woman shrugged. "Most likely the electrics are out, but it has the manual crank. It could be modernized quickly if her mechanical systems are right."

Paya asked, "Is it safe?"

She shrugged, giving us all a toothy smile. "We could send Frizzy up in her to see."

I almost growled at the woman. McGrath just chuckled out when Ange started to open her mouth to defend me, "I'm just teasin'." Then after a pause added, "Mostly."

Then she said, "We'll know more after I get a look at her. But my suggestion, lookin' at the condition, would be to keep what ya have."

Then Paya shot her an almost coy look, her signature crooked smirk on her face as she asked, "After you get a look at her? That means you'll take the job?"

The woman gave a smirk of her own, looking as though she had been caught with her hand in the cookie jar. "Don't be lookin' all smug like that just because you're cute. I'm particular about how a job is to be done, and I don't cut corners. You don't know what yer getting' into hirin' me. Just ask Brent. I'm not the nicest person to be havin' around."

Both Mr. Hastings and I snorted at that. Then the bloody woman had the audacity to grin and wink at me. She was amused I was put off by her. Oh, how I hated McGrath.

Paya held out a hand and said, "I think we'll take our chances with you."

They shook, then McGrath offered a hand to Angie and shook. She turned to me, and I was going to be the adult and shake when she offered. Instead, she spun her hammer in her other hand like a pistol and slid it into her belt loop then turned back toward the lift and said, "Be a girl and fetch us a fizzy?" Graaaaaah!

Brent looked at Paya and said, "My condolences on your selection of renovation contractors, I must be off to another meeting. We'll check in on progress from time to time to give guidance."

I heard a snort that echoed in the lift as McGrath said, "That was good, Brent, I didn't know you could be funny."

The man almost growled and then stalked away in a huff. As much as I disliked the handywoman, I couldn't help but be amused at how easily she got under the skin of the stuffy man who was likely to make the entire renovation a living hell for my bosses.

When he was gone, she poked her head back out into the corridor. “Those drinks aren't gonna be getting' themselves now.” Then she popped back into the shaft.

Angie sighed and looked at me and whispered, “Just humor her. I'll make it up to you. We need her.”

I stomped off, feeling every inch a petulant child.

To my chagrin, we learned that McGrath had to sell her truck a year ago to pay some bills. So I was assigned as her driver whenever we needed to go out for supplies that others refused to deliver for us. It seemed that everyone in the area seemed to share my opinion of the abrasive woman and most wouldn't work with her, except other contractors who all seemed to have an odd sort of respect for her.

She found sub-contractors with reasonable rates in the area who jumped at the chance to work with her. They all seemed to excel at their jobs even though they mostly charged half the going rates, though nobody worked even close to the ridiculously low ten pounds an hour she herself worked at.

I was starting to see that for how heartless she seemed, she absolutely loved what she did, and attacked it with a passion that rivaled Paya's for the Flotilla. More than once I caught her with her hand laying on some portion of the building needing repair and whispering things like, “It's ok darlin' we'll get ta ya soon.”

She was such a confusing person to me. How could she treat inanimate objects better than the people around her? Well not so much people, she acted more like an instructor to all the people from the Flotilla, who became her own personal army for demolition, cleaning, sanding, and other tasks. She always had a smile and kind word for all of them, especially the children, teaching everyone the proper techniques and how to use the tools correctly. And when Steph's kids, Wil and Natalie, were around she simply lit up and taught them how to use tools to help out.

It was just every other human being not associated with the project, or me and Hastings, which she seemed to take joy in tormenting.

There were times I had to spend more time with the woman than I wanted too at low tide, waiting for her vessel to float again so she could get tools or supplies or just go home. I learned she lived on the boat, the Deirdre, though nobody was allowed on it. Which just made me insanely curious of course.

That brings us to today, she had spent an inordinate amount of time in the middle of the main corridor on a ladder, where the ceiling was arched, examining blocks on the ceiling and some at the walls by the floor. She had looked deep in thought.

She came up to me at the end of the day. I was covered in sweat and sawdust since I had been tasked to cut trim for the doors in the building that day. She sat down beside me on a sawhorse and took her work-gloves off, tucking them in her belt.

She said almost in embarrassment, "So, Frizzy, could I be

imposin' on ya for a favor? I need to get to the Royal Library Archive before they close at six, and the busses can't get me there in time. I can chance my life by lettin' ya drive me there."

She was a taskmaster in the renovation project, and she had strict rules which she also applied to herself. She worked from nine in the morning until five at night every day like clockwork. It would take an act of God to make the woman leave the job site a minute early. It was a hell of a work ethic and something I grudgingly respected. This wasn't just some lackadaisical project to her. She took the Steinberg more seriously than breathing, just like Paya did.

So I understood that if she needed to take off early to get to the Royal Library Archive in time, it would never happen in a million years. I was sort of intrigued. What business did she have at the Archive? June and Vanessa's sister, Fran, worked there part time; she was having a torrid love affair with the books there.

McGrath didn't strike me as the studying type. I cocked my head. But then again, she had to learn all the tidbits about history that she shared with everyone on the project. I admit, they were sometimes fascinating facts.

I had to ask, "What do you need to do there?"

She cocked an eyebrow and asked quietly, "What? You don't think someone like me would be goin' to the Archives? I can read ya know."

Whoa, ok, that was odd, she wasn't being snarky, she seemed

actually put aback. I shrugged and clarified, "No, I'm just curious."

She shrugged and hopped up on her feet, pulling her gloves back out, and she actually slapped my arse with them as she said, "Just need ta do some research." I blushed for some unfathomable reason.

This was the first time she had asked anything of me that didn't pertain to the job, and she wasn't too aggravating about it except for the snipe about chancing her life. So against my better judgment, I said, "I guess I can do that." Then I warned, "But one crack about my driving and I'll throw you out of the vehicle."

She gave a super toothy grin. "Done and done, your driving almost throws me out of yer vehicle anyway."

I gruffed in exasperation as she walked off calling out, "Five o'clock everyone, put down yer tools, and I'll see ya all bright and early tomorrow."

After we got all the people from the Flotilla situated in the rental vans for the return to the dock, I took the fiery Irish woman to her destination. I went to follow her into the library when I parked on the curb by the large unassuming building near the Chelsea College of the Arts. My curiosity was getting the better of me.

She stopped me with a look, and a held a palm out as she got out. "Thanks, Frizzy, I can find my own way home." Then she just strode off with the pleased, smug look on her face, that I have come to associate with her. I watched her walk toward the building's entrance, and not for the first time noticed how unfair it was she was so toned and had a nice arse to boot.

Then I snapped back to reality and made an exasperated sound at being dismissed like I was nothing but a taxi driver. To hell if I ever did her a favor again. I kept glancing in the mirror as I headed away, curiosity burning.

So there I was the following morning, fuming at the girls as we met in the pilot house of the Persephone, over McGrath's treatment of me. "I swear, one day I'll snap. Crack. I'll kill her and rent a wood chipper over in the next county."

Paya put on an adorable pouty face and held her arms open. I grinned, rolled my eyes and sighed and stepped into her arms. I always blushed being this close to the dishy woman. But her hug did make me feel a bit better. She released me and said, "Just think, when the job is over, you'll never have to see her again."

I gave them both a manic, toothy grin at that, then she added, "But you have to admit, she is exactly what we needed to get this job done. I can't believe how much she has accomplished so far, and the people of the Flotilla are just beaming with pride knowing they are helping to build their own future flats."

I gave a grudging crooked smile and said as I waggled a finger in warning, "Yeah yeah, fine whatever. But if you tell McGrath I agree, then you'll have a date with the wood chipper too." Angie snorted, and we exchanged grins.

A bit later, as I approached the Hammersmith, I caught a glance of the Deirdre sitting on the silt as the tidal swell was slowly creeping its way back up to her. I parked on Lower Mall and looked around in confusion. McGrath was always sitting on one of the benches along the walk here, waiting for me, looking at an imaginary watch on her wrist.

It was Friday, we had a lot to accomplish before we called it a day. I didn't have any running to do for the girls that day so I was tasked to the annoying Irish arse. And I was loathe to admit to her that I actually liked helping out in the renovation. I never worked much with my hands before, and it was sort of gratifying in a way I can't fully explain.

I stepped out of the vehicle and walked to the edge of the promenade as close to the Deirdre as I could get. I didn't see any movement in the low windows of the upper cabin. I glanced around again, reaching absently for my mobile in my back pocket to call her when something caught my eye at the bridge.

Sitting on the bank with her back to the stone foundation of the north tower, was the missing handywoman. She was looking across the water as it made its slow, crawling approach up the silty bank. She was lackadaisically skipping stones across the Tames. She looked deep in thought and so... sad.

I started to walk that way but stopped. Would she want me intruding on what seemed a private matter? I just watched her a moment longer, understanding the need to get away sometimes, and I respected that even if I didn't respect the woman. Hell, I knew the need all too well, it landed me on the streets, which was in many respects, still an improvement on my situation.

I turned back to the truck and got in then rang her up as I watched through the windscreen. She looked down at her pocket. Looked up to the clouds, then tossed one last rock as she stood and started walking my way pulling out her mobile and answering. “What's up, Frizzy?”

Rrrrr. Here I thought she had depth for a moment. I snapped, “I'm here, where are you?” As I watched her grin at the phone then look toward the lane.

She said, “Look East.” Then she started waving and bobbling her head around as it was on a swivel. I didn't see any of that thoughtfulness or that sadness I had thought I saw at a distance.

I sighed and rolled down the window and waved back. What the bloody hell is wrong with me? I know it just eggs her on when I acknowledge her. I said, “I have better things to do than wait on your arse. Let's get a move on.”

She deftly climbed the retaining wall and over the railing and stomped her work boots, getting the silt and sand off of them before getting into the truck. It seemed she had more respect for it than for me. Still, it was courteous.

I asked as she shut the door, “What were you doing out there with the tide coming in?”

She looked down at her hands and started rubbing the side of one. It was the first time I saw the woman look anything but one hundred percent cocky. She looked almost, I don't know, vulnerable for a moment before she straightened and gave me a toothy grin. “Just had some things on mahy mind.”

Then she looked around the cab. "What? No coffee? What kind of runner are ya?"

I huffed as she grinned at getting a rise from me and I said through gritted teeth, "I'm not 'your' runner." Stressing the word your. Then said, "You want coffee, get it your damn self you wanker."

Her grin didn't waver, and I saw a twinkle in her eyes. What was wrong with the woman? I swear my anger entertained her. Then she bit the tip of her tongue, her grin turning into a smile I would have crawled through shattered glass to see if it hadn't come from her. "Well, then lass. Shouldn't you be drivin' us to a coffee house then? Mahy treat. Well, actually it's the money the Flotilla has been payin' me, so I should say, Miss Doshi's treat."

Ok, that was different, I have been the one having to get her drinks and meals for the past three weeks, on the Flotilla's account. It was the only concession McGrath would take above her meager hourly rate which she wouldn't allow Paya or Ange negotiate higher to reflect her worth.

She seemed adamant and a little forceful about her rates. There was something going on there that none of us understood, but the woman, who never spoke of herself or her past, was tight-lipped about any reasoning behind it.

We actually got more out of Mr. Hastings on his weekly visits to check out the progress we had made and to verify its historical veracity. He usually stormed off in a huff after just a few minutes with McGrath.

We found that her father had died of cancer a year ago, he had smoked like a chimney, and she took over the family business afterward. She had lived on the Deirdre with her father, and Connor McGrath was apparently twice as infuriating as his daughter. Hastings painted him as a devil tongued Irishman who was a true believer in hand tools over power tools. Of working with his hands. It sounded to me that the stuffy bureaucrat had a grudging respect for the man.

Apparently, Connor always believed he knew better than the OHP when it came to working on the historic structures in the borough. A nasty habit his daughter seems to have inherited. The man failed to mention that McGrath always wound up being right, though, she always had some obscure tidbit of historical information to support her claims. So I assume it applied to her father as well.

I remember hesitating a moment at the revelation about her father, and pulled out her card again and looked at the name Connor crossed out on it. She used his cards? Hadn't she said she had to sell her truck to pay bills about a year ago? Around when her father died. Coincidence?

I also wondered if that's what she did at the Royal Library Archive, research history. I had to stop myself from asking Fran if she knew what materials McGrath was looking at there. I didn't need to be a nosy snoop about.

I nodded at her and couldn't help but smile, saying, “True. I guess I can say the same thing about everything I buy since the

Flotilla pays me."

She nodded sagely and quipped, "Yes. And they are apparently paying you right now for sittin' here doin' nothin'."

I muttered under my breath as I started the truck and pulled out, flipping off the driver of the vehicle honking at me as they slammed on their brakes to stop from hitting us, "I don't care if you are twice my size. One of these days... you won't even see it coming."

I looked over, and she was practically hanging off of the handle above the door, eyes wide. Why did everyone seem to have the same look when riding with me? I yelled out the window when a bloke honked at me when I turned in front of him onto a side street, "Learn to drive you plonker!"

She said, "Jaysus. I believe you. Cept it'll be yer drivin' that puts me in mahy early grave."

I looked over at her and glowered. "What's wrong with my driving?" She was reaching a hand over toward the steering wheel, and I glanced froward and pulled us back into our lane. The driver of a passing car glared at me.

McGrath looked infinitely pleased by that, and I huffed out a breath through my nose in frustration and accelerated. That wiped the smug look off her face. Shite! I slammed on the brakes, our tires screeched a little, and I whipped us over to the curb at a local coffee house. Whew. I had almost passed it.

Before I could say a word, she had the door open and was sliding out, muttering to herself, "Decaf. I'm awake." Then she looked in. “Sit tight, try not to set your hair on fire, and I'll be right back.”

I flipped her off. She grinned and shut the door. I really hated the person I became around her. But she was just so bloody frustrating. I was never so crass around anyone else. Well, unless they teased me. But I was done being a target for others, that's why I ran away from home. I had a right to stand up for myself, didn't I? That's what Angie has taught me.

A minute later she came out with a tray with two drinks. She slid in, placing the tray on the dashboard as she made a show of fastening her seatbelt and testing it... twice. Smartass. Then she handed me a cup, saying, “Black, one sugar, no cream.”

I blinked. How did she know how I took my coffee? I knew she took her's black, and the stronger, the better, but she had no need to know mine. I took a hesitant sip and singed the tip of my tongue, but it tasted right. Huh. I nodded and said, “Thanks.”

She sipped her coffee with a half smirk as I put mine in the cup holder. She said as she looked over the lid of her cup, “You're welcome, Frizzy. And here we find ourselves again watchin' you gettin' paid for lazin' around, doin' nothin'.”

She barely got her coffee secured and grabbed the handle over the door when I had us screeching back into traffic with her chuckling over her success in pissing me the hell off. I glanced down at the coffee. She knew how I took it. Maybe she wasn't a total lost cause.

When she got her breathing under control one eye squinting at the road as she held onto that damn handle, I asked, "It would be sort of crucial to know exactly where we're going for supplies. I mean, I can just drive us all the way up into Wales otherwise." I turned my head to her.

She reached a hand toward the wheel again, her eyes wide and on the road, I glanced forward and swerved back into our lane. A car horn was blaring as a vehicle passed by the other direction. I rolled down my window and yelled out, "Learn to drive, tosser!"

McGrath muttered, "Jaysus." Then exhaled and said, "Tom's. We're goin' to Tom's. That's much closer than the land of windbags."

Tom's? That's the other direction. It is her preferred hardware store in the area instead of the big box home center a couple miles away. I actually find the place charming. It screams of a bygone era where everyone knew everybody from a neighborhood. I could imagine the butcher and chemist shooting the breeze with Tom as they got supplies for their weekend home repair projects.

Warmth. That's what it was. The place had a warmth you would never expect in a Wyvales or Homebase.

I was actually impressed with the number of the little hole in the wall places she has me drive her to, to get all manner of hardware and supplies. It almost felt like I was moving in the circles of a secret society.

I saw an opening between a lorry and a van and did a u-turn. Sheesh, why did the lorry driver swerve? McGrath was gnashing out something between her teeth that sounded Gaelic to me as she practically hung off the handle. She must have agreed with me, that lorry driver needed to stay off the road if he couldn't drive right.

I found a place at the curb by Tom's, and McGrath was breathing hard. She glanced at me then grabbed her coffee and gulped it down before taking the time to speak. "You're a crazy one, you are."

She slid out, and I followed her. "What's that supposed to mean? You're the crazy arse Irishwoman." Then I narrowed my eyes. "Are you complaining about my driving again? If you are, then Paya and Ange be damned, you can walk."

She turned to me as I reached her side under the shop sign proudly proclaiming that we were at "Tom's Ironmonger's." She said in that more Tweedledee accent she got when she was being a condescending bint from hell, "I wouldn't be doin' that now. Yer drivin' is..." She searched for a word and smiled, tilting her head as she finished, "Lovely." Stretching it into three syllables like she had done with Hastings. Then she fluttered her eyelashes to punctuate the backhanded slight.

I exhaled as I shook my head while she held the door to the shop open for me. I passed by, muttering to her, "There isn't a word in the dictionary that can convey the depth of my hate for you."

She chuckled, and I hid a smile as she said with that silly inflection, "Ahh... there now. We'll make a proper Irishwoman outta ya yet."

She grabbed a trolly from the front, and we started down the tight aisles which had floor to ceiling shelves with all sorts of home and garden supplies, tools and hardware, including things I had no clue as to their use. Again it struck me that a lot of the items looked like they were from another time with their faded boxes and antique looks, mixed in with modern plastic blister packs.

She called out with a smirk, "Jaysus, look at this shite. What self respectin' ironmonger has such a pitiful array of wares?"

From the next aisle over I heard a now familiar gruff old man responding in his Cockney accent, "Only a fuckin' eejit would..." Tom paused as he stepped around the end of the row of shelves and saw us. He looked down in embarrassment, and said, "Miss Lenore. Beggin' your pardon. I didn't know you were with the poxy leprechaun." The brawny and bald grandfatherly man winked at me as he lazily looped his thumbs under the straps of his work apron as he stepped up.

I snorted. She thumped my shoulder. Ow. I don't think she realizes just how strong she is.

He leaned in and the two of them hugged, slapping each other on the back like teammates at a football match. Sometimes the woman seemed so butch to me. She asked, "You got mahy message?"

He nodded then gave me a head bob of greeting. I beamed at the old guy. He looked back at her and replied offhandedly, "I've got it on a flatbed trolly in the back, I'll bring it up and help you load out. I'll have Gerald deliver the lumber before noon."

She nodded. "Thanks, Tom." Then he was off, and we moved through the shop.

She absently grabbed various fasteners and hardware as we went. She paused and pulled the trolly back a step, almost causing me to crash into her back. I was about to snap at her when she turned back to look at me. "Did ya say that Steph's wee ones would be with Ange at the Steinberg today?"

I nodded, wondering where that came from. She looked back at the shelves then hesitated, then seemed to make a decision and I cocked an eyebrow at her when she grabbed two packages off the shelf.

Huh. Every time I'm dreaming up a new way to make her disappearance look like an accident, she goes and does something thoughtful like this.

She actually looked embarrassed as her face reddened around her freckles a touch. She said, "You can be shuttin' up now, Frizzy."

I fumed, and she grinned, and we moved on. She said, "You forgot your work gloves again now didn't ya? I din't see them in the truck."

Ok, now I was embarrassed. She drills into every one of us who helps out in the renovation that we wear proper safety gear including gloves, hard hats, and safety glasses. And in the rare case she pulls out a power tool, earmuffs.

I've had to wear her spare gloves on occasion when I forget mine on the Persephone. I feel like a little kid when wearing hers since my hands are so much smaller. It is something I can't fault her on. She seems to genuinely care that everyone is safe on the job site which she rules with an iron fist and that intimidating hammer hanging on her hip.

She must have seen my meek attempt to not look her in the eyes. She shook her head and stopped at a shelf with various work gloves as she let out an exasperated breath. She dug around in the stacks and pulled out a couple pairs and made a show of putting them in the trolley.

She said, "Green. Keep a pair in the truck for the next time ya forget."

My favorite color? I nodded absently as I looked at the back of her head as she continued toward the checkout. Her pixie cut was just touching the nape of her neck, right at a small tattoo of a white flower, no bigger than my thumbnail, which I had been dying to ask about. I cocked my head and asked, "Green?"

She nodded without looking back and said like I was a simpleton, "Yes, ya know, yer favorite color?"

How did she know that? I glanced at my green shirt. Now that I think about it, most of my shirts are green, and my iPad and iPhone covers are green. My keychain is green. Ok so she's not clairvoyant, I'm just that transparent. Still, she had taken the time to notice the little things like my coffee and my color preferences.

Maybe she wasn't as... "Come on Frizzy, get a move on. The

Flotilla doesn't need to be payin' ya to just stand there daydreamin'." Graaaah!

She paid for the two packages and gloves first, with her own lolly. Then she moved aside, and I paid for the rest and the lumber order with the Project's card. I saw two younger men loading boxes into the back of our supply truck as I glanced out the windows.

I kept looking at her. She seemed distracted today. I kept catching that shadow in her eyes until she schooled herself again. I wondered if I should ask. Not that I cared or anything...

We loaded up and made good time back to the Steinberg. I think I beat my record. She seemed oddly distracted, looking out the side window as I drove. She even forgot to grab the handle and mock my driving. She was absently picking at her lower lip when we pulled to a stop.

I was oddly relieved when she slipped back into slight slinging banter when we got out to unload. Others came out to get the supplies from the back. When we got in, our arms full, I had to grin at Angie and what she called her Roos as they sanded some kick boards installed in the almost completed lobby.

They looked far too cute with their little yellow hardhats on.

Ange wasn't even their mother; well not yet anyway as she and Steph are talking about tying the knot; but she has a better relationship with those children than my parents ever had with me before...

It was plain to see to anyone with eyes, that she loved those children like they were her own, just like she loved Steph. I envied what they had, a family, a happy family.

The kids turned to see us approaching, and they squealed and ran toward us. I couldn't stop grinning if my life depended on it, they were too dang cute.

McGrath squatted and set down her armload of items so she could grab the munchkins into a hug as they chimed out in cute voices, "Aunty Builder." Then they detached and went for my legs as I giggled at them, "Aunty Lenny."

An excited Wil blurted out to us, "Mummy Kanga says we get to work with you for the whole day! There's no school today!" Angie was their kanga, and they were her roos. I had melted into a puddle of "dawww" the first time I heard it.

Then I melted from the radiating heat the first time I saw Stephanie and Angie's eyes meet when I was introduced. Those two have a burning passion that is tangible in the air when they are close together.

Then McGrath reached over to one of the big plastic buckets she had carried in and said, "I have somethin' fer ya. Mahy wee foremen need to make the proper impression on their workers. You need ta project the right image. So here are you are."

She held out the overly cute little tool belts that had actual real tools in them that were just scaled down for a child's hand. The tiny hammers were adorable, so were their answering squeals as the Irishwoman lashed the belts to their waists while Ange beamed at them.

Those little ones seem to always be squealing, but not in an annoying way, they are just too happy all the time. It always made people around us smile when they heard it. I had to cover my nose to stop from snorting when Natalie took out the little hammer from one of the pouches and slid it into the loop on the belt just like McGrath does.

Then the evil woman glanced at me and blushed at being caught gushing over the little ones, and she said to Ange, nudging her chin toward me, "Here she is again, getting' paid to be standin' around doin' nothin'."

She gave me the toothiest grin as I shot her a death glare. Angie just rolled her eyes at our antics then said, "Thank you, McGrath, that was sweet."

The musclebound handywoman shrugged, blushed, and looked away. She just picked up the supplies again and started down the hall toward the lift she had been working on steadily for the past week. It was looking almost usable now, though she still hasn't given the all clear to test it yet.

She called back to the children as she walked, "It just wasn't proper fer mahy foremen to not have their own tools. And wee ones?"

They called back in unison, chiming out like the schoolchildren they were, reciting a lesson, "Sand with the grain, not across it."

She bobbed her head emphatically in satisfaction without looking back. I hustled after her with my load. I wondered what task I'd be assigned to today between running messages for the Flotilla. I hoped it wasn't lath and plaster. Please don't be lath and plaster.

She dropped her things and looked over at me as I placed the supplies beside hers. She said, “You best help the Hamptons with lathe and plaster in flat 104.” Buggar all.

I sighed heavily, and she looked back at me as she released the cage door on the lift. She cocked an eyebrow and asked, “What? They are well meanin', but they don't have yer eye for consistency. They need proper supervision.”

I blinked. Wow, that was almost a compliment. I didn't know what to do with that. I hid a blush. I was finding that I really enjoyed working with my hands to actually create something. People were going to be living here, and I had helped make their home.

She snapped me out of my thoughts as I started to turn as I nodded. “And Len, let down your hair every once in a while would ya. You don't need ta be so high strung all the time. Enjoy things while ya can, ya never know when time is up.”

Then she just turned back to her work. I kept my eyes on her for a five beat before hustling along. She hadn't sounded snarky just then, her tone was almost profoundly sad. I worried as I made my way to flat 104. What had been weighing so heavily on the redhead all morning? Maybe I should ask at lunch. Or maybe Ange knows. I don't know why I care.

I never got a moment to ask, and lunch was ordered in for the crew.

We all cheered at the end of our break when a smug looking McGrath had us gather around the end of the main corridor, and watch as she stepped into the lift, closed the cages, then hit the controls and the noisy elevator whirred its way up. She stopped it and then used the old manual crank controls to lower it back down to demonstrate she had the beast fully functional.

Ange bumped my hip with a smug 'told you so' look on her face. I glanced up at her and said, "Fine whatever, she knows her shite." Then I sighed and handed over a quid for swearing when the roos were within earshot.

She took the next fifteen minutes, giving everyone rides on the gothic looking lift. She called Ange, the roos, and me over as the last group. She pointed out the intricate cast iron decoration of the open shaft. "You notice how it looks like a big birdcage? And the wings are drapin' all along it like the outside of the buildin'?"

I took the time to really look at the cage and realized that she was right. I mean I noticed it was pretty fancy for this just being an apartment block, all shiny black painted cast iron, but I hadn't realized how it tied in with the exterior. There was a theme winding its way through the structure.

My eyes snapped to the ceiling, to the new crown moldings she had started bringing in one stick at a time. I didn't know where she had been getting it since I was the one driving her around for supplies. Those same wings adorned the molding, interspersed with wreaths like at the main entry. Wherever she found the stuff, it was beautiful. It all looked hand carved as each wing seemed unique like there was no repeating pattern.

The carvings went a little past the seam each time, overlapping it, giving the illusion that it was one single long piece going down the entire corridor. At the rate, the stuff was trickling in. We wouldn't have all the moldings up until close to the end of the project.

Even Mr. Hastings said the OHP had no problems with the molding selection. It was consistent with the era, either carved hardwood or plaster moldings, and he was impressed she had found some that kept with the theme of the building.

We had said goodnight to McGrath as she went to walk the couple blocks home like she did every night. Ange glanced at her mobile while I crouched for the munchkins to climb on my back with their tools in their belts, which they refused to take off, poking at my ribs.

She locked up the building, and we stood on the walk as she said, "Steph should be by any minute to pick us up, she texted that work went a little long."

"Nonsense, I can give you and the troublemakers a ride home," I offered.

As the children cheered, she blurted, "No!" Then she calmed herself and said plainly, "I'll not be risking my Roos in a vehicle with you at the wheel."

I narrowed my eyes at her as the little ones chimed out in

chorus, “Awwwww.”

I shook a finger at her. “I'm not that bad. Seriously.”

She cocked an eyebrow in challenge. “Oh really now rocket woman? Do you think you could drive us home without donating to the swear bucket?” She made a good approximation of McGrath's accent as she asked, “Or will ya be puttin' the wee ones through college by tha end of it?”

I shook my head but couldn't help smiling at her. Fine whatever, maybe it isn't every other driver on the road. There may be one or two little points I can improve upon in my driving. I muttered, “I really hate you sometimes.”

She chuckled and ruffled my hair like a kid and kissed the top of my head. “Tough, we all love you.” I blushed profusely.

The cute girly tone of Natalie's voice came from where she was hoisted on my back, “What mummy Kanga said.” Wil, always following his big sister's lead, said, “Yeah.”

I looked back at her with a grin and a wink, saying, “You little rats, you're supposed to be on my side.”

Little Nat got a look on her face that would have rivaled Paya's indignant expression she displayed when you didn't cave to her will in two seconds, not that anyone could resist for longer than that, “We're roos, not rats.”

I nodded and said, “You're right!” Then I started hopping around as they held on tight and giggled in glee. Then I settled as Stephanie pulled up in their vehicle. Their vehicle... I shook my head and said, “You two need to tie the knot, Boss. I don't know what you're waiting for."

She tore her eyes and smile off of the waving woman in the SUV and blushed profusely. I smiled. Steph was the one thing that could crack her air of invincibility. She said almost shyly, "I will, you wicked wretch. And don't call me Boss. I just... she's..."

I finished for her. "Crazy about you."

She sighed like a lovesick girl and then said, "Come on Roos, let's hop to it."

I grinned at her change of topic and squatted for the kids to hop off. My back ached a little, they were getting so big. They literally started hopping to the vehicle, saying, "Hop, hop, hop." It still amazed me that there actually were people out there who had happy childhoods.

Ange said, "Bye brat, see you Monday."

I nodded and watched as they loaded up. Stephanie looked out the window at me, the side of her face ticking from the nerve damage, and waved a farewell to me. I waved back as they pulled away, little hands waving back at me through the back window. I kept waving.

I'd see Ange tomorrow, not Monday, and she knew it. She and Paya were workaholics, and they always checked in on the weekends even though they knew I had their Flotilla for them since I lived on the Persephone.

I stood there a moment and felt oddly exposed and... alone. I pulled out my keys and headed to the truck to go... home. I smiled. Yes, the Persephone felt like my home now.

Chapter 3 – Drunk

I awoke to my mobile ringing, it was the Queen Space Vampire's Death March from the Heartsong Warriors movies. But I had assigned that to... McGrath? I saw the red numbers on the clock on the counter at the kitchenette and squinted, my eyes blurry from sleep. Just past two in the morning?

What the bloody hell did she need this late at night? I stared at the mobile on my nightstand, I should just let it go to voicemail. I didn't need any abuse just then. But then curiosity and something akin to concern came over me when I remembered the odd cloud that seemed to be hanging over her at the Steinberg earlier.

I scrubbed my hands through my hair vigorously and growled out an "Arrrrrrrgh!" Then I grabbed my mobile and accepted the call. "This better be good, or they'll never find your body."

A man responded in a deep, gravelly voice, "Umm... hello? Is this Lenore Statham?"

I sat up in bed. Why was a man calling me from her phone? Then I wondered, does she have a boyfriend? She never talks about her personal life outside the project.

I said carefully, "It is. Can I help you?"

He asked, "Do you know an..." There was a garbled sound like he was doing something on the phone then finished, "...an H. McGrath? You're number one on her speed dial."

I swung my legs quickly over the edge of the bed and to the

floor, feeling like I needed to bolt at a moment's notice as my heart started pounding. I blurted out, “Has something happened to her?”

He said in an off-put tone, “Not unless you count being too shitfaced drunk in my pub to walk straight. We shut down ten minutes ago, and I can't make sense of what she's saying enough to get a home address, or I'd have already shipped her home in a taxi. I would have kicked her arse to the curb when she backed down Dickerson earlier, but that man is a class A arsehole, and she may have made him piss his trousers.”

I exhaled deeply. Part of me relieved she wasn't hurt or anything. Then a familiar anger started rising in me. An anger I thought I had left behind when I ran away from all I knew just before my seventeenth birthday.

McGrath was drunk. I had had enough of drunk people to last a dozen lifetimes. The selfishness and the... I calmed myself, reminding myself that McGrath wasn't my father. People drink, it doesn't mean they all abuse alcohol... or their families. She had seemed like something was haunting her all day. But whether I liked it or not, she needed my help just then.

I felt angry for some reason, maybe because my opinion of her had just dropped a bit, and that made me upset. I centered myself and replied, “Ok. I'll be right there, what's the address?”

After I rang off with the information in hand, I dragged myself up and just put a coat over my pajamas. I ran my fingers through my hair as I trudged out and down to the deck, then hopped over to the dock and to the truck. I got my twisting locks into some semblance of control and went to pull up my scrunchy and paused, damn, I didn't have one on my wrist when I slept. I sighed, I wasn't walking all the way back up to the pilot house to get one.

I looked like shite and was still in my PJs, my wild, curly hair wasn't going to detract much from the overall picture. Then I was on my way to Jack's Pub. I liked driving really late at night. London never slept, but at night, there were a lot less bad drivers on the streets. I only had to exchange the finger twice with other drivers and roll down my window once, to curse at a guy who deigned to honk at me because he couldn't be bothered to get out of the way.

I found the address, it was in the shadow of the Hammersmith, maybe eight blocks from where McGrath anchored the Deirdre. I paused as I shut off the engine. The man had said she was H. McGrath. I wonder what the H stood for. Heather? Helen? I chuckled... Hag?

No, hag she was not. She may be a lot of things, but the woman would be drop dead, eye gouging gorgeous if it wasn't for her poison personality. I'd have found myself trying hard not to stare at the woman if every fiber of my being wasn't restraining me from justifiable homicide. And I don't normally prefer the butch look, though on her it just made her look more feminine, even with the preponderance of muscle on the woman.

Hannah? Hope?

I walked up to the door of the pub, a red neon sign proclaiming they were closed. I tried the door, and it opened.

The place was dimly lit and looked like any other English pub. I saw a thin and tall man look up from cleaning the bar. He nudged his chin to the back, and I saw a familiar redhead slumped against the wall in a chair at the back table. Her eyes were closed and appeared to be sleeping. I gave the man a wave and made my way through the maze of tables to the Irishwoman's side.

I looked at her a moment and saw something I had never seen before, she looked to be peaceful and sort of vulnerable. Not this larger than life caricature of a person she went through great effort to project. I had intended to kick her foot to wake her, but I couldn't bring myself to do it. Instead, I leaned in and whispered, "McGrath, come on, wake up. Time to go home."

She just moaned a little and turned away slightly in her sleep. I smiled and reached out to place my hand on her cheek, my fingertips tickled by the shaved hair above her ears. Her skin was deceptively soft. I said a little louder, "Come on McGrath, time to go."

Her eyes fluttered open, and she didn't move a muscle, her eyes taking in the pub. Then she noticed me when I pulled my hand back. She looked almost ashamed as she slid back in her chair then her eyes went wide with recognition and her cocky expression returned.

She said in a slur with a self-satisfied smirk, "Frizzy. See? I told ya ta let yer hair down. It looks good." I didn't know what to say to that, and she added, "Are ya in yer jammies?"

I blushed. "Shut up, lush. Come on, time to get you home."

She sobered a little at that and then nodded once and tried to stand on jellied legs, only to flop back into the chair. She looked suddenly sad as she looked up at me. "Come now Lenore, have a drink with us. We're celebratin' the one year anniversary of me Da's death. God rest his soul." She looked toward the bar. "Barkeep!"

I held a hand up toward the man as I looked at her, realization dawning, and my anger at her was quickly replaced with an empathy I never thought I could extend to the abrasive woman who was the bane of my existence. She was in mourning, and it didn't look like she knew how to do it properly. I could see the endless pain in her eyes.

I exhaled then shook my head once before leaning down and wrapping an arm around her waist. "No, come on, time to go. We can talk about your father later. This nice man needs to close up his pub."

I heaved, and she stood on swaying legs. I grabbed her bag and helped her to the door where the bartender met us. Holding up a mobile and sliding it in her bag. He held the door for us, and I gave him silent thanks. He winked at me, and I assisted a staggering McGrath out then down the way and into the truck.

By the time I made it to the driver's side, she was passed out against the window. I drove carefully to the Deirdre. I drove painfully slowly like Paya and Ange did, as not to wake the sleeping woman beside me. How could they not go insane driving like this? I could probably run faster.

I glanced at the woman who looked so very small curled up against the door. Hillary? Hollie? Our checks were always made out to McGrath Handyman Service, so I didn't know if Angie or Paya even knew. It was going to drive me crazy. I wondered if it was on her contract paperwork.

I pulled to a stop on Lower Mall and hissed, "You've got to be frickin' kidding me." Low tide.

I glanced again at the woman, she seemed to be having a nightmare of some sort as she mumbled and seemed to flinch away from something. I reached over and rested a hand on her cheek again. Then couldn't resist running my fingers through her silky pixie cut.

I sighed in resignation and started the journey back to the Flotilla. The stairs were going to be a real buggar.

***

I woke up to a sound in the cabin. I glanced over from where I slept in the chair beside the bed and saw McGrath pulling on her boots. She froze when she saw my eyes on her. She looked... embarrassed.

I sat up and immediately regretted it, my joints ached. I do not recommend sleeping in an uncomfortable chair. I pushed some hair out of my mouth and blinked blearily at her and accused, "Just going to sneak out?"

She looked down and then continued pulling on her boot. She

stood as she said, “I've made enough trouble fer ya.” Then she looked down at her hands and said in a resigned tone, “I'll understand if the Flotilla will be wantin' a new general now. I can make some suggestions.”

I stood and stretched out my legs, working the kinks out as I said, “You're a bloody git, aren't you.”

She blinked and her mouth worked but then she prompted slowly, “Beggin' yer pardon?”

I chuckled at the unflappable McGrath in all her... flapped? Glory. “You must really think poorly of us to believe that we'd be upset at a woman grieving the death of her father.” I added, “Annoyed as sin to be woken up in the middle of the night to retrieve your drunk arse, yes, but upset, no.”

She stared at me in incomprehension, but not for the reasons I believed when she asked, “You... know about me Da?”

I shrugged. “Not much. You told me last night it was the anniversary of his death.”

She said only, “Oh.”

Then she looked around suddenly and asked, “How did I get here? We didn't...” She swung a finger back and forth between us.

It took me a moment then I barked out a surprised bark of laughter and said, “Oh God no.” Giving her a sour face.

She had an indignant and embarrassed look on her face before her cockiness returned, “Alls for the better, you wouldn't have been able ta handle me.”

Without missing a beat, I shot back, “What? You mean between cleaning up the puke on my floor before passing out again in my bed? That's a real prize there.”

Her eyes went to the floor. “I didn't?” Then she looked up at me. “Dear Lord, Fri... Lenore, I'm terribly sorry.”

I gave a toothy triumphant grin, “Don't be, now I have something to hold over your head, and I have seen the great McGrath at her most vulnerable.” It wasn't lost on me that she had used my actual name.

Her embarrassment transformed, and she shot a toothy grin back at me. What was she on about now? I almost died of embarrassment on the spot when she prompted, “You think I'm great?”

I exhaled and looked down, shaking my head as I muttered, “How much do I loathe thee, let me count the ways.”

She chuckled like she had won something and said, “Well I'll be getting' out of your way now. I rightly apologize fer you seein' me at mahy worst. Sorry 'bout yer floor.” Then she added after a hesitation, “Even mussed up like that, yer hair looks better down like that.”

Dear Lord, why was I blushing? I fought the urge to reach up and touch my unruly curls. I exhaled and chastised myself inwardly for what I was about to do. “Wait. I'll give you a ride home. It'll be a pain to catch public transit on a Saturday unless you take the tube on the Piccadilly. And you need to get something in your stomach, believe me, it's empty now.” I made a sour face.

She sighed and said, “Again... sorry.”

Then she looked to start to decline, and I added, “Besides, you owe me. Tell me about your father, Connor.”

She stood there staring at me with a glare that would have melted glass. I had been glared at by the worst of them, so her's was inconsequential. She muttered, “Fine. Now I know why your hair is so curly, it's tryin' ta get away from you.”

I grinned in triumph. Hallie? Harper? I shooed her. “There's should fresh coffee on a timer in the pilot house. Let me get changed.”

She had a grin on her face, and I snapped out, “What?”

She shrugged and said as she looked out the windows to the rest of the Flotilla, “You never said you lived on a boat.”

Ok, why the hell was I blushing again? I shrugged and said, “You never asked.”

She passed through the doorway and into the pilot house as she said, “Touché.” The smell of freshly brewed coffee wafted into the room as she shut the door, making my stomach gurgle.

I glanced back at the door and found my hand absently touching my hair. The wench was trying to confuse me, and it was working. What did I care what she thought? I growled and stomped to the loo for a quick shower.

After cleaning up, I stood in front of the mirror as I dressed and wondered, not for the first time, if I had any redeeming qualities. I knew I had an abrasive personality, but that was the defense mechanism I had built up over the years as I grew up. I guess I looked ok-ish. I hated my hair, though my friends always said they'd kill for curls like mine. Even Angie. But not Paya, she loves her long black hair, which is straight as a board and gorgeous, I'm so envious.

I can't tell you the pain in the arse maintaining hair that wants to curl around and do its own thing is. I like my particular shade of brown, it borders on a chestnut, so that's the one good thing I can say about it. Maybe I should try straightening it one day.

I paused. What the bloody hell was my obsession with my hair today? I looked at the hair dryer in my hands and decided against plugging it in and just combed back my damp hair. I looked at myself and made a silly face. It looked so much better with most of the curl out of it, so I think my friends are all on drugs. This artificial straightness will give way to the unruly curls as it dried.

I started to grab a scrunchy for my wrist but found myself looking back at the door, then decided against it. I don't know why. Helga? Heidi? What the hell was her name?

I dressed in my lazy day clothes, just jeans, and a tee before I grabbed my jacket and stepped out into the pilot house. McGrath was leaning on the console by the big ship's wheel, supporting her weight on her arms as she looked out across the Thames.

Dear lord, I'd be staring at that arse of hers for hours if she wasn't the most aggravating person in the world. But seriously, how was it even fair to get her height and an arse that could barely be contained in the heavy denim she preferred?

I saw two mugs of coffee on the little conference table in the back of the wheelhouse. I grabbed the closest which was full. I sniffed and took and experimental sip and sighed out an appreciative, “Ahhh... just right.” That hit the spot. She turned around at that with a cocky smirk.

I cocked an eyebrow in challenge at her as I gulped the almost scalding coffee down. Her eyes moved from mine to my hair, and her smirk became almost smarmy as she turned back to the river. She asked, “You can pilot this beast?”

I shrugged though she couldn't see. “I do alright with her, but Angie is the master of the Persephone. We take the barge out on the waterways once every other month to exercise the engines. It is sort of an event with the residents here, you should come sometime.” I paused, realizing what I had said. Too late to take it back now.

She didn't seem phased as she just said without looking back, “I'd love to.” I relaxed for some reason. Hattie? Hazel?

I blurted out in frustration, “What does the H stand for?”

She turned back with a look of confusion painting her face. She was looking at me like I was off my trolley. “The letter?”

I growled, was she being dense on purpose. I prompted, “Your name. What does the H stand for? It's driving me over the edge here.”

She narrowed her eyes. “How do you know about that?”

I shrugged. “The barkeeper last night said your mobile

belonged to an H. McGrath."

She looked at me and her bag on the conference table near me. She seemed to be contemplating something. "I guess I owe ya that much, But if it gets out, I'll be huntin' ya to the ends of the Earth."

I swallowed, she looked serious. I nodded, and her glare turned playful as her Tweedledee came out to play, "Of course, you'll be owin' me the story of yerself, lassie."

It was my turn to freeze. I didn't talk about my past, even to Angie and Paya, though they know the basics. You can't say no to Paya once she turns on the cute. I swallowed hard. This Irishwoman was going to tell me the story of her father, so it was a fair trade. A secret for a secret.

And I needed to know what the bloody H stood for!

I nodded, and she gave me her signature, "Lovely."

I put the mug down and prompted with an arched eyebrow. She stepped over and shrugged and said, "Hunter. It stands for Hunter." She looked at her hands and picked at something imaginary on the side of one as she explained, "Me Da wanted a boy... he got me instead." She shrugged.

I found I was smiling at her. "Hunter. I think that's brill." It fit her, and she seemed to hate it. Was it because of what she said, her father wanted a boy but got her? On her, it wasn't masculine at all, it just... fit.

She huffed and said, "I'll be thankin' ya to be callin' me, McGrath, please."

I said, “Why start now? Until now I've been calling you...”

She interrupted me by holding up a finger, a special finger, a middle finger. And we shared a chuckle. Which struck me as strange. I was actually having a good time with McGrath? No, with Hunter. I'm sure things would change back to normal when we started back to work on Monday.

The weekends don't count, as shields are all down, there's an unwritten rule about that somewhere isn't there?

I said with a little resignation coloring my tone, “Well let's go get you fed and back to the Deirdre. You can share your story along the way.”

I grabbed my bag from the hook by the door to my cabin, and we paused as the door opened and Paya stepped in. “Hi brat, how's...” She trailed off as I looked over at her. She was looking between Hunter and me with my wet hair. She got an inappropriate smile on her face as she almost skipped over to the coffee maker to pour a cup. “Well helloooo McGrath. How are you this wonderful Saturday morning?”

Bloody hell! She thought we had...

Hunter was quick to say, “I dropped by to borrow your runner this mornin', last minute supplies.” She shot me a pleading look. She was embarrassed about the real reason she was here.

I stuttered, “Ummm... y-yeah.”

Paya cocked one of her perfectly sculpted brows. She wasn't buying it one bit. She knew the Irish handywoman's strict work rules as well as I did. When five o'clock rolled around each weekday, then it was hammers down. No exceptions.

I gave my Indian-Brit boss a pleading look. She brought her coffee cup up to her lips and took a sip as she regarded us and wondered what we weren't saying, she no longer had bedroom suspicions, which had made her all too happy for some odd reason. She gave me a small nod then placed the mug on the table and asked, “Have you two eaten breakfast?”

I sighed in resignation. “I already offered to feed the annoying bint.” Then to Hunter, I added, “She has this odd fixation with making sure everyone has enough to eat.”

McGrath chuckled at me and then said to her, “It's true. Frizzy here already mandated a meal before anything. I think it's admirable you look out for others this way Miss Doshi.”

Oh dear lord, I could see Paya's head swelling from where I stood, we didn't need to be reinforcing it. She looked at me smugly as she said to the redhead, “Why thank you, McGrath.”

I snorted and pointed a finger. “Don't get all smarmy now woman. You pay her to brown nose.”

This got an explosion of giggles from Paya as she stepped to my side and kissed my cheek. “You're such a brat. Now shoo. I'm meeting Ange here in a few minutes. The city is trying to throw up some new roadblocks on the renovation, and it is time for me to start making waves again.”

I blushed and grinned at her as I said like I was reciting lessons, “Yes Paya.” The city didn't stand a chance against her.

She was all too pleased as she said, “There's a good girl.”

Then to Hunter, she said, "Keep her out of trouble?"

The traitorous woman replied with a smug, "I'll do what I can. But the woman is trouble incarnate ya know." They shared a chuckle at my expense. Hey, I thought Paya was supposed to be on my side. The traitorous wench. She smiled at me cutely. Oh, ok, I'll let her get away with it.

I grumped out, "Come on you surly leprechaun." Their chuckles increased as she followed me out the door into the chilly morning air.

Chapter 4 – The Deirdre

We opted to go through the drive-thru at the Golden Arches, she didn't want to speak about herself out in public, and I didn't blame her because she reminded me this was a tit-for-tat situation and that I owed her my own story.

How much I actually shared was going to be dependent on how much she shared with me. I was quite confident that the only personal information she would get from me was my middle name since I seriously doubted she was going to tell me much. She had something against me, and I figured she had already opened up as much as she was likely.

I almost missed our turn but was able to slide between two oncoming vehicles to get onto Rutland, horns blazing, then veered off onto Bridge View toward Lower Mall. My red-headed nemesis was hissing the whole way. I shot her a look as she virtually dangled off the handle which she had dubbed the "Jaysus Christ Bar."

I asked between gritted teeth, "What?"

She gave a nervous grin. "I just thank mahy lucky stars I don't have a heart condition."

I sighed out in my defense yet again. "My driving isn't that bad."

With her eyes wide in disbelief she countered, "Says you."

I cocked an eyebrow as I looked at her and challenged, "If I'm such a bad driver, then why have I not been in a single accident nor been ticketed since I got my license? Tell me that, Red."

In response, she reached over toward the wheel, and I looked back at the road and yanked the wheel to avoid the oncoming vehicle and got us back into our lane as his horn blared past. She chuckled out nervously, "Divine providence? Or because you've been blessed by the fact that those retreatin' around ya are much better drivers than you."

I exhaled and relaxed my shoulders, I'd never win at this. There was a one hundred percent chance that that woman would never agree with me on anything. If I said water was wet, she'd say it was as dry as the Sahara. I started revisiting my wood chipper plan in my head when we pulled over to the curb near the Deirdre. The tide was coming in, and she had just started to float again.

Curiosity was killing me, and I asked, "Deirdre?"

She responded quietly, a forlorn tone to her voice, "Twas me Ma's name, God rest her soul."

I blinked then looked from the boat to her. That was another little piece of information I didn't know. She was alone, like me. Well not like me, as my parents were still among the living, but I would never claim them as my own. I left, and will never look back. Never.

I didn't know what to say, but I didn't have to since she took the bags of food, and the drink carrier, and slid out of the truck. I looked back through the window to her boat.

The Deirdre looked to be a cross between a small Dutch barge and a houseboat. I wouldn't have known a barge from a wayward walrus just a year and a half ago, but once Ange found me and made a home for me at the Flotilla, I've had a fascination for barges of all types.

The boat was painted that bright green that caught my attention the first time I saw it. It may be because green is my favorite color. The paint was old and peeling away, and it was painted red below the waterline. The steel hull needed a good cleaning.

The stern of the craft had, in huge gold scripted letters, Deirdre, painted on it, with it's Hull Identification Number in white block letters below it.

Every available spot outside the deck-side cabin was covered in stacks upon stacks of old doors, windows, and old lumber covered in tarps with narrow walkways between it and the metal railing that circled the boat.

It would have looked like a floating junkyard if it hadn't been so organized, and everything didn't look so vintage. The low, squat cabin ran half the length of the fifteen-meter vessel and had a rounded roof. The bridge was slightly higher, giving it an unobstructed view around the boat.

The elongated portholes along the length of the boat told of another level below decks. They made me I absently wonder how much room she had inside. The most prominent thing about the boat were the big banners on either side made of tarp-like canvas which had her company name and number on them.

Besides that, she was a boat of modest character, and if it weren't for the color, I would never have noticed it out on the waterways of the city. But I was dying to gain entry to it. Nevertheless, it was forbidden fruit. McGrath had been adamant all these weeks that I pick her up on the roadway. And I don't believe it had anything to do with the tides since she had mentioned in passing a couple times that nobody was allowed on the Deirdre.

However, here I was, invited onboard. Wait... she was going to kill me wasn't she? They'd never find the body, and she'd whistle while she worked. I was startled out of my wandering thoughts by a knock on the windshield. "Lenore? Are you going to sit out here all day dreamin' or are you comin' in?"

Oh. I had to get a handle on my fantasy life. It wasn't lost on me that she had used my name again instead of Frizzy, so I muttered to her in kind, "Keep your panties on, Hunter." I grinned at her death glare and slid out and locked the truck.

I followed her to the railing at the stone retaining wall at the river's edge, which ran the length of the promenade. She looked a little nervous for some reason. She was always so confident and take charge, it was sort of odd to see her hesitant and... human?

She looked around, then squatted to run her hands along the underside of the lower railing, where it connected to the stone retaining wall. A moment later she pulled out a long metal pike with a hook at one end. It had to have been two meters long. She swung it out and hooked a counterbalanced gangplank on the

Deirdre. She pulled, and it swung down smoothly. I could see the ropes working on the counterweight system and grinned to myself. Of course, it operated smoothly, it was McGrath's of course.

She tucked her pike away in it's hiding spot, exhaled audibly, then offered an ushering hand. “After you short stuff.”

I muttered to myself, “Not all of us are blessed with Amazon proportions.” I tried not to grin at the chuckle behind me as I slid over the railing and walked across the gangplank to the waiting deck of the floating shamrock of a vessel. It had a springy bounce to it as it flexed and swayed with my weight. It was a far cry from the stout ramps we used on the barges of the Flotilla.

Once I had my feet on the deck of the boat, I felt the reassuring subtle movement beneath my feet which I had come to associate with home, with safety, the feel of a ship on the water. I turned back to watch McGrath make the crossing, with a familiar smug look on her face and an extra bounce in her step to make the gangplank flex and rebound.

She hesitated again once she stood beside me, staring at the cabin, then she nodded almost imperceptibly like she were making another decision and said, “Come along then Frizzy.”

I would have pushed her overboard if she weren't holding my breakfast and my stomach wasn't threatening to eat me from the inside out. “Frickin' leprechaun Amazon.” She got a bit more bounce to her step at that. I was clearly amusing her.

There was barely any place to walk as we made our way to a

door. The stacks of doors looked more like treasure now, old solid wood doors that had hand carved reliefs, judging by the unevenness of the surfaces. They whispered of a bygone era where craftsmanship won out over utility. A time long lost to generations like mine.

I paused at a window frame that had what looked to be grape vine carvings crawling all over it and across panes of glass which were so old they were bubbling and warping a bit, creating the distortions I have come to associate with antiquities. I could barely make out the faded paint colors and imagined what it had looked like when it was displayed in all its glory before being left behind by time like this.

I stopped at that revelation and spun back to look at all of the relics from another time. That was it... this was a graveyard of sorts. She was preserving their memory by not letting them be lost forever. Yes, that played with the feelings I got from her whenever I caught her speaking to the old woodwork in the Steinberg.

I think... I think I understand her now. At least a tiny part of her, and what drives her to be so rigid and particular in her work.

I glanced back at her and froze. She was studying me as she waited by the door, holding it open and not saying a word. I felt myself blush a little and said, "Sorry, all of this stuff is beautiful. Antique." I hustled toward the door as I added, "I had thought it was just all junk until I got closer."

She nodded slowly, and I tried not to meet her eyes as I

passed through the doorway, ducking a little until I took a step down and found adequate headspace. She said as she closed the door behind me as I gazed at the space in shock, “I can't bring myself to let them be thrown inta the skiffs at the job sites. So I take them away with me. Mebbe I can find new homes for them, and breath new life inta them. They were someone's blood and sweat and tears, and deserve better than ta be relegated to history, as an artifact of our past.”

I tore my eyes from the space to look back at her. She had such a wistful look on her face. I silently wondered if she realized how beautiful her face was when she wasn't being a bitch queen. Then she shrugged and seemed to pull herself back into the present. “Well, that's neither here nor there. I'm ready to eat mahy own shoes. Let's have our breakfast and then I'll share what I've promised, but no more.”

I nodded in acceptance of the terms, I wasn't too keen on sharing with her either, and I was bloody ravenous. She led me through the space to a large table. I was so busy gawking at everything around me that I almost didn't notice the long boards she quickly covered on the table with a drop cloth. I narrowed my eyes at the end of a piece of blank molding that had the beginnings of the carvings of wings on it.

She gathered some wooden hammers and chisels and placed them in a big wooden box with a carry handle and placed it on the floor by the grand table. I saw a large board formed into a crescent shape leaning against the wall, and it had similar carvings in it. She covered that with another drop cloth before turning around and sitting at the table without a word.

I looked back at the covered molding and asked in a distracted voice, "Are you actually carving the..."

She slapped a breakfast sandwich wrapped in yellow paper in front of me at the table and demanded, "Sit Frizzy. Not a word or I'll be thankin' ya fer the ride and sendin' ya on yer way."

This took my attention off of the woodwork, and I groused at her, "Why do you have to be so infuriating? Did I wrong you in another life or something?"

She chuckled and took a big bite of her sandwich and challenged through a grin with her mouth full, "Can't ya take it?"

I growled as I unwrapped my egg and cheese delight, "I can take more than anything you can bring to bear, you demented shamrock."

Her smile was gone instantly, and her face was suddenly serious and inquisitive, "Why don'tcha tell me about it."

Whoah that felt like she had just maneuvered me into a trap somehow. My mouth went dry. I paused... wait, this was just a distraction. I accused as I pointed my hash brown patty at her, "Nice try, you plonker. You owe me a story."

Her smirk was back, being caught as she shrugged and sipped from the paper coffee cup as I looked around the amazing space again.

It looked almost like something out of the roaring twenties in the Americas. Everything I looked at seemed to be made of carved wood, either in an art deco style or in spectacular nature and animal expositions that seemed to weave their way around the immaculate room.

From the tigers peeking out from the vines that seemed to climb the fluted support columns to flow into a canopy of carved ceiling tiles, to the sharp lines of the high rise that framed the windows which had a spectacular view of the Thames.

The huge space seemed to serve as the living room, kitchen, and dining room. It was bigger than my entire cabin and pilot house combined on the Persephone.

Even the table we sat at was amazing, the legs had carved vines and snakes holding up the huge single slab of dark wood. Wait, were the legs carved like ostriches and alligators?

The door frames of the three doors at the end of the space alternated between geometric art deco carvings and more of those spectacular animal laden vines. There were animals from all parts of the world represented in the display as they peeked out from huge carved leaves or climbing flowers that seemed to organically flow around the space. Even the furniture and baseboards were carved with idyllic scenes or geometric patterns which seemed to flow effortlessly together.

The whole place smelled of wood oil and wax. The carvings looked meticulously maintained and were shining brightly in the natural light coming from the skylights. They were obviously well loved.

I was at a loss for words, and I glanced over at the

Irishwoman who seemed to be watching my reaction intently. I nudged my eyes toward the bear that seemed to be holding the roof up in the corner, and she smiled almost bashfully as she looked around and shrugged, "This is how me Da taught me to work with mahy hands."

I blinked in shock and found myself blurting out. "You did this?"

She shrugged again. "Some. Mahy stuff is mostly in the other rooms. Da was a master woodworker. He tried ta teach me the proper respect for the wood and the tools. He showed me that if ya lay yer hands on it, ya can feel what is livin' inside. Ya just have to coax the life into it with the tools, the wood knows what it wants ta be."

I just absorbed what she was telling me, it was almost poetic. Then looked over to the drop cloths and accused, "The crown moldings at the Steinberg?"

She narrowed her eyes and warned, "Don't go opening yer fool mouth about it."

I shook my head, not breaking eye contact, I wouldn't show weakness to anyone, especially not to her. I nudged my chin toward the large curved board she had covered, "And that?"

She finished for me, "Is none of yer business." We sat there, eyes locked for five long heartbeats before I nodded once.

I almost groaned when she grinned in triumph and gave me her drawn out, "Lovely,"

I took another bite of my food as I shook my head. "I don't

know why you're hiding it, it is amazing work."

She shook her head and explained in her serious tone, "That takes away from the majesty of the wood. It deserves to be appreciated for what it had hidden in the depths of its grain, not for the one who coaxed it out."

She said matter of factly, "You'll be getting' a thumpin' from me if this gets out. This is why I don't let anyone on mahy boat."

I mumbled back, "As if you could take me." Ok, whatever, she'd snap me like a twig. All the muscles in my body combined would fit in one of her biceps. But I don't take kindly to threats, even from a gorgeous Amazon.

She chuckled out as she sipped her coffee. "Dream on little fuzz-top. You're like a wee kitten battin' at a wolf." Then she paused and cocked her head as I started ramping up my rage. "You really should let your hair down more often, it truly looks better this way, Len."

Just like that, all the wind was taken from my sails, and the heat of my rage for her changed to a different heat as I blushed. I absently touched my rapidly drying hair as the loose curls slowly tightened into the bane of my existence. "I... you... shut up."

She chuckled with that aggravating smirk of hers on her face. Then she slapped her hands palm down on the sturdy table, making a loud thwacking sound. "Right then. I'll tell what I promised as I give ya the grand tour of the Deirdre, me Da's pride and joy."

I stuffed the last half of my hash brown into my mouth and

wiped my hands on a napkin as I stood and gathered our trash. I looked around for a bin, and she took the bag from me and tossed it into a wood-fired stove that stood in the middle of the space facing the seating area. It was such an amazingly cozy place for how big it was.

She stepped to one of the doors and opened it, but didn't step in. She just stuck her head in and said, “The master suite. Me Da's. God rest his soul.” I looked in, and it was covered in carvings just like the main room. On one wall was a carved bookcase that covered the entire length of the room. The titles I could read from where we stood were all about architecture, history, and woodworking.

It was as immaculate as the other room. I had expected the inside of the boat to be just as cluttered as the exterior. I hadn't expected this level of tidiness nor the amazing wonderland that was displayed through all of the carvings.

She pulled back and shut the door before I could finish taking in the four carved dragons that seemed to be winding their way to the top of the four post bed, their wings spread wide. I realized she hadn't moved into the master suite after her father passed. She stepped away and tapped the second door and said dully, “This is the head.”

She moved on to the third door and held it open for me, making an ushering motion. I stepped into a corridor which was just wide enough for two people to pass by each other. It reminded me of the corridor on a sleeping coach on a train.

To one side were the elongated windows lining the corridor, on the other, carved wood panels and adornments. It was just as amazing as the rest. Each panel seemed to depict a different scene, and they were divided by more of those climbing vines and flowers that seemed to fill every nook and cranny, making the space one organic, uninterrupted sculpture.

I mentioned it as we moved along. "It is like each panel is its own story." We were half way to the end, and I noticed the carving style seemed different here than at the beginning of the hallway.

She nodded and said in a faraway voice, "They are. They're memories. Me Da's diary..." She indicated the other panels as we walked. "And mine." Her... memories? I looked closer at the scenes. There was one of the Hammersmith with the Deirdre herself floating on the Thames. The grain of the wood looking like the currents hidden below the surface of the waters.

We got to the end of the corridor and there was a door to some stairs going up, I knew that would be to the wheelhouse. There were some blank panels there, and chunky wood dividing them. I absently touched one and smiled. A future memory. The story hadn't come to an end yet. She turned to the last panel where a door was inset.

There was an arch of wood around it. Carved with teddy bears and wood blocks at the bottom, giving way to dresses and shoes, to books and then to nothing but blocky, uncarved wood. A story to be told. I realized what I was looking at as she opened the door. This was a master woodworker documenting his daughter's life. I knew what I would see when she motioned for me to step in. This was her room.

There were some carvings adorning her room, but a lot of it was a blank slate, only one wall had carvings and a crown molding of wood blocks and bassinets. The lack of carvings suddenly felt so plain and felt oddly empty in comparison to the rest of the ship.

My brow furrowed, and she must have read it. She smiled sadly. "He said it was mahy story to tell. I work on it when significant things happen in mahy life."

The room was clean, though not as immaculate as the rest of the place. It felt cozy and lived in. There were books and old newspaper clippings neatly stacked on every horizontal surface. They were the same type of books as in her father's room. There were architectural and history books.

A newspaper clipping on the dresser beside me had some architectural features circled in red, of a building above the picture of a politician from the early 1920s.

I cocked an eyebrow when I noted a cheesy lesbian romance novel sitting on her nightstand. It was one I had read not long ago. I glanced back at her. So she played on my team? How was that even fair to the rest of us, having to compete against her for women? I mean come on, look at her, then look at me. Why would people go for a cheeseburger when they could have filet mignon?

She prodded me back to the present with a, "Come on then, let's get below decks, and I can share mahy story with ya while I work on the motor. I'm getting' close to makin' her operational again. Da was never able to finish before..."

I just nodded at her, not knowing how to respond. It was... different... seeing her vulnerable again. I never would have thought the woman had any weaknesses. Well except the one in her head after I clubbed her for treating me like her personal assistant. I was Angie's assistant. Not a pushy handywoman's.

We left her room and went through the door at the end of the corridor. There was a small vestibule which had stairs heading up, and a smaller set of steep stairs heading down.

I followed as she slid a handle on the wall and I heard the coughing and sputtering of a generator coming to life, then lights flickered to life in the hold below. I looked back, realizing that we hadn't had any power before that, all the rooms were lit by the windows that lined the length of the upper deck and strategically placed skylights.

I don't know what I expected belowdecks, but it wasn't what looked to be one huge open space. Unlike the upper deck, it was just the spartan metal walls of the hull and metal supports holding up the upper deck. There were more stacks of doors, windows, crown moldings, and carvings of what looked like ornate spindles and balusters from stair railings.

There was sawdust everywhere and tables with half done carvings and stacks of fresh lumber. Old school hand tools were hanging everywhere and were scattered along the various tables and workspaces. I had to grin, there was a couple power saws too, a bandsaw and a table saw. She tried to do without power tools in the restoration project we were working on, but it seems that she still needed to use them occasionally.

She draped a drop cloth over the nearest table that looked to have some planks clamped and glued in the shape of the curved board in the main room above. She tucked what looked to be a newspaper clipping under the cloth as she looked back at me.

What was she hiding from me? I had already sussed out that she was the one providing the crown moldings for the Steinberg.

She muttered, "Pay no attention to that man behind the curtain." I had to grin at the Wizard of Oz reference, but now I was dying of curiosity as she led me past the table. I started to reach over to peek, but she anticipated that and said without even looking back, "That's a good way to lose a finger... at the shoulder."

Alrighty then. I dropped my hand to my side and followed her to the very back of the space. We stepped onto a metal grate, and she stopped, turned to me and wiggled her eyebrows and pushed a lever attached to a railing up and with a burbling blurp of water, I heard the bilge pumps start up. I looked down into the recessed area and saw a couple inches of water shimmering at the bottom. We had something similar on the barges at the Flotilla, just not as industrial and steam punkish looking.

She pulled a section of the grating up, and it hinged over and clanged back onto the floor. I glanced down the hole and saw an engine no bigger than what was in my supply truck. I expected something, I don't know... bigger? Like we had on our barges. But then again, ours were two or three times the size of hers, and we had two engines in each.

She must have read my expression and said, “Fifty-five horsepower diesel, same as you'd find in'a farm tractor I s'pose. Don't need much to get her movin', and even then she's in no hurry to get where she's goin'.”

Her voice drifted a bit into the melancholy of a dream that lay just beyond reach. “Da was gonna fix her so we could sail her back to Ireland to visit me Nana on the twenty-first anniversary of when me Ma died givin' birth ta me. He says Nana had promised to give me somethin' fer Ma when I became mahy own woman. A promise Ma put her to on her death bed.”

I swallowed as I tried to gauge her age as she started making her way down into the engine compartment, her feet splashing in the little bit of water being pumped out, which had seeped in from God knows where. No matter how well sealed a boat is, water always seems to find its way in.

I asked quietly, “How old are you, Hunter?”

She stopped moving then said as she regained her wits and grabbed a hand towel that was on top of the engine and wiped her hands nervously, “Twenty one just a week before your Flotilla found me. Hand us a seventeen-millimeter spanner would ya?” So he had died before they could sail across the St. George...

I looked over to where she indicated, her head and shoulders sticking out of the grate opening. There was an old open galvanized steel tool chest. I started digging through it and found the wrench she required and handed it over. Before I released it to her, I asked, "How long has it been since you've been back home?"

Her Irish accent wasn't really pronounced unless she was remembering things long past, teasing me or was playing with her Tweedledee. So I imagine she had been in London for quite a spell.

She ducked down and started attaching a bulky cylindrical mechanism to the engine, tightening bolts with the supplied wrench. "I am home."

I exhaled and groused, "You know bloody well what I mean, woman. Stop trying to get a rise out of me?"

I could almost hear her smirking, it was obvious since she didn't look up as she worked. Then she said, "Comin' on ten years now. I mean, we visit both my Nanas from time to time, whenever we got a chance. But it's near half my life now since Da and I sold our house and sailed the Deirdre ta England ta make our fortunes." She hesitated and asked the air, "Has it really been almost half mahy life?"

She looked up at me and paused, then said in a serious tone, "I'd've gone back ta visit after the funeral, 'cept we were barely makin' ends meet before... and I had to sell the truck fer Da's service. He deserved better than a pauper's burial."

That struck me like a blow across the face. That's why I was driving her around? Because a girl who lost her father had sold her transportation to bury the man who raised her? She exhaled and prompted, “Flat blade screwdriver.”

I dug one out and handed it to her, and she said without looking at me as she attached a wire to the unit she had just installed. “I don't make a habit of airin' mahy personal laundry. I'd appreciate if it didn't leave the boat.”

I nodded absently, not knowing what to say. She said in a chipper tone, “If I can breath life back inta this beast, I'll keep our promise.”

I smiled at that.

Then she added, “Ol' Deirdre has been down coming on two years now. I've been fightin' the borough on mooring rules. I haveta move her soon, or she'll be impounded.” Which wiped the smile back off of my face.

And then she went about telling me all about growing up on a boat. About all the places they had gone and seen before settling in London, in the shadow of the Hammersmith. Where her father had become the bane of the Office of Historic Preservation's existence.

There wasn't anything he didn't know about woodworking or architectural history, and she followed in his footsteps. He was the one person she looked up to, and that shaped who she became. And now she is carrying on the McGrath tradition of being the thorn in the side of Mr. Hastings and the borough council, because, “Someone has ta keep them honest.”

She shared far more than I thought she would. I was feeling... not so hate-ish about her when she finally wound down. Then she pulled herself out of the pit, wiped her greasy hands on the towel and slammed the grate back in place.

She asked as she put the tools back in the toolbox, “What say you Frizzy? Care to try to breathe some life back into the dead?” My newfound respect for her as a woman evaporated when she called me Frizzy. I growled at her, and she gave ma a cocky wink. I could feel a blush spreading on my cheeks and had to stop myself from nervously running a hand through my curls. I nodded, not able to find my voice. What the bloody hell Lenore? Kick her arse!

She reached past me, leaning in so her face was right beside mine. My breath hitched, and I could feel her warm breath on my neck. I swallowed as gooseflesh rushed down my neck and spine. Then heard some clicking and turned to see her flipping a breaker switch and then she pulled back and started toward the stairs. “Come along then. Ya owe me your story.”

I swallowed again, bloody hell it was hot down there. The fresh air above decks sounded good. I pulled my wits about me and ran after her like a puppy on a leash. Fuck. I was seeing her as a real person now... a real sexy person. But that warmth washed away as she said, “Your real story, not the shite yer feeding Paya and Angie.”

I asked as I headed up the stairs after her. “You can be a right wanker at times, you know that?"

She nodded as she headed up to the wheelhouse. "So I've been told on numerous occasions. Most recently by you... in multiplicity."

I grinned at that and said in a pleased tone, "Good, the message is getting through then. I thought I was being too subtle."

She exploded into a surprised laugh at that and held the door open at the top of the stairs for me. I had to squeeze by her, our bodies brushing. I could feel the heat of her body and the solid muscles hiding just under her shirt. I was acutely aware of how small I was compared to her and how strong and... female, she was.

If I didn't know any better, I'd think she was doing this on purpose. Just another way to tease me. It wasn't funny. Someone like me would give anything to be with someone like her, but without the caustic personality which came with her of course.

I started breathing again when I stepped into the wheelhouse. It wasn't anything special, it was just a smaller version of the Persephone's, but built for utility. Glass all around gave a good, unobstructed view for navigating.

The only concession was the ship's wooden wheel, which was carved to look like an octopus wrapped around an anchor. The eight legs stood out as grips to turn the wheel itself. It was pretty bloody cool.

McGrath stepped beside me and slipped a key into a panel and turned it, then indicated the big red button above it to me. "Want the honors?"

Ok, I smiled at that. She was going to let me try to start the ship named for her mum. I stepped quickly beside her and nibbled my lower lip as I looked at the red button. I looked at her and squinted an eye and pressed and held.

I heard and felt the wheezing whup whup waugh of the engine turning over. And just when I was about to give up and release the button, it rumbled to life in a familiar deep growl of an underwater exhaust system.

I released the button and we cheered, and she pulled me into a celebratory hug. Good lord was she hot. I closed my eyes a moment as I caught her scent. All sawdust, grease, and soap. It was a scent I caught from her from time to time, and I associated it with the woman. It wasn't unpleasant in the least... quite the opposite.

She released me, and I started breathing again. I didn't know when I had stopped. Then she flopped into one of the three chairs that were secured to the floor in front of the panel as she turned the key off. She was nothing but grins as she motioned a hand over to another chair and said, "Now that that is sorted, ya owe me a story. Best be quick, it's comin' on lunch soon."

I blinked. Had we really toiled away most of the morning below decks? I hadn't planned on doing much more than a drop and run with her earlier, but I'm oddly glad I hadn't. She has turned out to be, much to my grudging admission, quite a fascinating lady.

Then my respect washed away as she added, “Let's start with your real name shall we Lenore? Statham? Really?”

I exhaled heavily. She was way too smart for her own good. I should have just left, but I felt oddly obligated now that she had opened up to me. Me, a girl she didn't even like or respect.

I started to deny, “I don't know what...” She pulled a folded up piece of paper from a pocket and unfolded it and handed it over. I looked down at the flyer. Seeing a picture of a younger and more naive me. Huh, I hadn't realized my parents even gave enough of a shite about my running away to have gone looking.

I asked as I looked at the generic wording. Have you seen this girl? Sixteen. Missing. Please call with any information. Lenore Guinevere Elgin. It had been a long time since I'd gone by Elgin. Where in the hell had she even found this? Colchester in Essex is quite a ways from London.

I had picked Statham on a lark when Angie had asked me my name when we first met in that alley in what seems like another lifetime ago. I didn't want to ever go back to Colchester, so didn't give my real name. The last movie I had watched before running away was a Jason Statham action flick. He was strong, a fighter, and not afraid of anything, everything I wanted to be. Everything I couldn't be when I cowered at home.

I stared at the flyer, then at her. Panic and an odd anger came rushing up, clouding my mind. She had known? For how long?

I turned and headed toward the door. “I don't want to play anymore.” She started to follow, but I spun on her. “And you can get yourself another dog to kick, I'm through. You better not tell the girls.”

She started after me again, and I slammed the wheelhouse door on her and stormed down the stairs, almost at a run, as the chilly fire of fight or flight coursed through my veins. My hands were shaking, and my breath came in shuddering gasps. It's what I did, I ran.

What if she tells them I had lied to them since the day I met them? They couldn't send me back since I was an adult now, but their respect was the only thing I had in this new life of mine. They had seen me at my worst and still took me in. I don't know if I could handle it if Paya and Ange turned their backs.

I virtually ran down the corridor and into the main room. Once I had exited to the main deck, I ran down the gangplank, hearing McGrath calling to me from the upper deck of the boat. “Lenore. Come back, talk ta me.”

I rushed to the truck and just drove. I didn't know where I was going, but I just needed to think. I screamed and slammed my hands on the steering wheel before holding it in a death grip, my knuckles whitening under the strain. The pain from the strike feeling far too familiar.

I just drove, and when my mobile chirped, I absently turned it off and kept driving. A little voice inside my head I hadn't heard for two years was whispering, “They'll know now, run. Running worked the last time.”

Chapter 5 - Running

The sun was setting, I had been sitting down the block from my old house, just watching, thinking. I hadn't even realized I was coming here as I drove, but almost two hours later I found myself parked by the primary school watching the home I had grown up in. But it seemed so surrealistic and almost artificial to me. It looked like any other home from the outside, hiding what really went on on the other side of that red painted door.

I wasn't that same scared little girl anymore. I was a new person, and the people who had helped me find my strength would hate me now once McGrath told them about my lies. I knew it was too good to be true. I had thought she had started... liking me. But she was just waiting to drop her bomb on me. I wish I knew what she had against me.

My fear turned into anger. How dare she snoop into my life. How did she know I was lying about who I was, and how the hell had she found that flyer? And why did my father even bother putting up fliers when I went missing? It isn't like he gave two shites. Maybe it was mum, or possibly he didn't want to look like the heartless plonker he was.

The sun extinguished itself on the horizon, and I reached for the keys to start the truck then paused when I saw some boys walking toward the house. I blinked when I recognized the tall one in their center. Robert? He had grown like a weed. He had been thirteen when I abandoned him and Christine. He had to be a head taller now. Taller than me. My heart thumped hard in my chest, my little brother was growing up.

He waved the other two boys off and then went up to the door and seemed to take a deep breath and steel himself before stepping in. I remember having to do that every time I came home. Preparing myself. I usually took two deep breaths before gathering enough courage to open the door and greet my parents.

As I just sat there contemplating how I had abandoned my brother and sister, a light went on in the upstairs dormer window which used to be my room. I had been the foil for my siblings, I ran interference for them. Without me there, they'd have to have faced the brunt of it.

I sat forward in my seat leaning into the steering wheel when I saw Christine standing in the window. Part of me was happy she had my room now. It had that window which I would use to... she climbed out onto the roof and sat, covering her ears to block out whatever was going on downstairs just like I did.

I turned on my mobile, ignored the various messages, then dialed 999 as I watched her. I gave an anonymous domestic abuse report to the dispatcher then rang off. I shut off the mobile and tossed it onto the dashboard.

Christine let go of her ears and looked up to the sky like I had done so many times. Wishing to be anywhere else. Wishing to be anyone else.

Why was she still there, in that house? She was eighteen now, and adult. She could get out of there and never look back. A light went on in the adjoining dormer and then I got it. She was stronger than me, she was staying for Robert, and I was a fucking coward. They were my responsibility, and I had abandoned them.

I started the truck. Here I was, running again. I drove slowly past the house, looking up at Christine, casting her wishes to the sky, keeping my face in the shadows. At the end of the block, I turned back toward London. Angie didn't need to think I was stealing the truck as well as lying to her.

A cruel smile crossed my lips when I passed a Bobbie heading toward the house. Take that Mitchell. It wouldn't do any good, but at least it would make my father be a little more careful for a while. It always did when someone called in about the yelling.

I thought about what I was going to do when I got back. I was a much stronger person than I had been when they found me, they taught me to be strong. I could remake myself once again, with this new identity I had shaped for myself. I wouldn't have to live on the streets this time.

I parked the truck and made my way to the pilot house of the Persephone. I fought back stinging tears. Oh, how I loved this ship and all the people associated with it. I packed a bag and was sure to take my emergency stash of lolly. I had taken to keeping a large cache of money in case I ever found myself in a situation like before, when I had been ill prepared. But never again, I would always be able to fend for myself now.

I paused as I looked at the bundle of cash. Had I always known I would run again? No matter how much this felt like home to me now. No matter how much I loved the girls and the people I surrounded myself with? Had my parents so utterly broken me that I believed that I could never truly be happy, never find peace?

I left my keys and my mobile on the conference table in the pilot house, let a hand drift out to caress the ships wheel. An image of an octopus and an anchor came unbidden to my mind, and I pulled my hand back and huffed in exasperation. I had let McGrath get under my skin while she was setting me up for a fall.

I took one last look around. I would miss this place, the Flotilla. Then I steeled myself and headed out into the world that didn't scare me as much as the first time I took a leap of faith, to try to reclaim my life, silent tears rolling down my cheeks.

I went to check the time on my mobile as I made my way toward the Tube and froze. I had forgotten already. Alright, getting a disposable mobile was one the first things on the to-do list in the morning. It still wasn't too late, the Tube would still be running.

I hopped the first train, not caring where it brought me. So long as it was away from the core and the Hammersmith. I looked at the map of the line on the wall, how far could I go? Hmm... Watford. Why not? It was just as good a place as any. An hour from London's core and Hammersmith. I could get a job there until I figure things out, maybe I'll head to Cardiff in a few weeks to make the new Lenore, three point oh. I have my new ID after all.

I tried not to think about what I was leaving behind. Unlike the first time, I was actually running from the people I loved. Well, that's not entirely true. I had abandoned my little brother and sister before. It seemed to be a pattern with me.

Chapter 6 – Frantic

I stared out the window of the pilot house of the Persephone whispering, “Speedy, where are you?” I turned when Tabby stepped in, letting in a blast of frigid air which carried the first wisps of snow as twilight started wrapping itself around the world. The cloudy sky was taking on a slight orange hue as the sun started setting beyond the veil of those clouds.

Her brow was furrowed in worry as she said to me, “Hiya Paya.”

Then she turned to the haunted looking Angie who was standing near me, gazing out over the water. As hard as Lenore's disappearance was for the rest of us, it hit her much harder. She felt as if Lenny were her little sister and she had somehow let her down. “Hey, Ange.”

Angie glanced over and offered her a smile in greeting as Tabby asked, “Any word?”

I still remember the frantic call from McGrath that fateful Saturday two months ago. It took a minute to calm her and to get her to speak plainly. Her slight Irish accents gets almost unbearably heavy when she gets emotional, which makes her hard to understand.

She explained that Lenore had run when she had asked about her at her place. She had shown her one of the fliers we had all seen almost two years back when we took her in. Len believed we hadn't found out who she really was and why she ran. We let her have that, she was flighty, and we wanted her to feel safe and loved around us. We knew she'd tell us everything when it was the right time.

I had blurted, “You know she's a flight risk woman, you could have been more subtle, McGrath.”

We had originally thought to help her to get back home since she was underage until our lawyers discovered that there were dozens of domestic disturbance calls to Lenore's house in Colchester over the years. She had all the telltale signs of domestic abuse. The way she held herself and flinched when anyone raised a hand to get something from a shelf.

She was just a year from becoming an adult, and since she hadn't shared her age with us or her real name, we could plead ignorance if it ever came up. We came to love her as our own flesh and blood in no time flat, she was smart, funny, sarcastic. Though she can't seem to grasp the whole driving without endangering all of mankind thing.

She has slowly grown into an extremely confident and self-sufficient woman. She shared with us her age on her eighteenth birthday. We knew it was only a matter of time before her flight instincts had settled down enough until she would talk to us and share her story with us.

She had been crushing on McGrath hard since the moment she laid eyes on the woman, I don't think she even realized it. But it scared her and caused friction between the two that was almost explosive. McGrath rose to the occasion and relished the battle. I had hoped that when I saw them together here that morning that they had finally buried the hatchet so to speak and gave into that volatile passion.

Our girl could do much worse than McGrath, who is fiercely intelligent and kind of terrifying in the same instant. But she has those smoldering looks that have even straight girls taking notice and getting warm in all the right places. Hell, she could make my knees a little wobbly with that smirk of hers, knowing she can back it up. And have you seen the muscles on that woman? It's no wonder Speedy is tongue tied around her.

It seems that McGrath was making a connection with Lenny and they were sharing their pasts. But then the Irishwoman pushed too fast and showed her the flyer, and Speedy's flight reflex kicked back in.

McGrath came to the Flotilla looking for her but the truck wasn't here, so she scoured some of the places she had been with Lenny to no avail. She finally gave up around ten that night and contacted us in a panic.

We all tried calling her and leaving messages, but her phone was off. We met McGrath here at the Persephone an hour later, and Angie had to cover her mouth to stop an anguished squeak when she saw Lenore's keys and the mobile on the table.

We checked her cabin, her suitcase was gone. She had run again. There was no note, no anything.

When we went down to the truck which was now here, the hood was still warm. We had just missed her. She could be anywhere. She had run over one hundred kilometers the first time. Now she was on the streets again. Angie had snapped at me when I voiced that, "No, not on the streets. She's grown much stronger and more capable now." That much was true. She'd have a plan, and that hurt a little knowing she never felt completely safe here.

The problem we had was that without knowing anything about her life before she had come into ours, we didn't have any insight as to where she would go. If you had asked me where she would run to, I would always say to Angie. But from what McGrath said, Len threatened her not to tell us. Did she really think we didn't know, that we would be upset somehow?

But then I thought of Stephanie, who had suffered through extreme spousal abuse, and she shared that Lenore likely thought we would feel betrayed and that would shame her. The victims of domestic abuse almost always blame themselves, thinking it is their fault. And that nobody would understand and would hate them for the things they did to hide it.

Was my heart supposed to hurt so much?

We hired a private investigator to find her so that we could talk with her, let her know we love her and support her and already know much of her past. The man was good and had thought of things we hadn't and was able to track her to Watford, where she had worked in a kitchen as a dishwasher for a couple weeks then moved on.

From there to Oxford where she helped out an elderly couple

with their farm for a week. But then she seems to have vanished, the McClintock Agency believes she may have left the country. They've put out feelers in Wales and Ireland since she seemed to be moving west, but they haven't heard anything back yet.

We found that not only had we come to depend on having Lenny in our personal lives, but things around the Flotilla had become quite hectic. I don't think she realizes just how valuable she had become to the Project. She was the best runner and assistant Angie could have hoped for, and now Ange and I had our hands full doing all the running, keeping up with the renovation, and battling the London City and Hammersmith borough councils. Not to mention providing transportation for McGrath.

I had finally just handed the keys to the supply truck to the handywoman as an indefinite loan until the Steinberg was finished.

McGrath had not been her confident self since Speedy bolted. She seemed unsure of her decisions and didn't fight with Mr. Hastings from the OHP on their demands much. I understood what was eating away at her. She was harboring guilt inside her that we couldn't assuage. The muscular woman had become part of our family, and my heart went out to her.

But her work ethic hadn't suffered. Angie, Tabby, and I have had multiple conversations about the blessing that woman had wound up being. Her combative and competitive personality aside, we couldn't have wished for a better contractor to head up the renovation. That became clear quickly. I doubt there is another person in all of London who had a better grasp on what was needed at the Steinberg.

She had this knack of inspiring all of the people on the Slingshot Program who would become the new residents of the apartment block when it was finished. She has instilled pride in the people for their own work and for the building. McGrath had a knack for finding the best job for each person and being patient as she taught them how to work with the tools and materials.

I'm pretty sure the children of the Flotilla, especially Steph and Angie's roos, have the Irishwoman wrapped around their fingers. She lights up when she shows them the proper way to use and respect tools. She has this almost Zen approach to the wood and materials that the children take to like ducks to water. Working with your hands is becoming almost a lost art, but she is introducing the children to the joy and pride that results from it.

We were only about five weeks from completing the renovation, and the Steinberg looked like a completely different place now. It was timeless now, right out of the pages of history, like it had stepped out of some Victorian romantic novel.

Tabs repeated herself, knocking me out of my thoughts and back to the present. “Earth to Paya. Any word yet?”

I crinkled my nose at her and reached out to take her hand for a moment to give it a little squeeze. “Not yet. She hasn't been answering her mobile so she may be in a dead zone on the road.”

Yesterday McGrath had come to us and said, “I'm going to

take the rail up to Essex Saturday."

Angie almost snapped her own neck, her head came up so fast when she realized what the redhead with that awesome hair was saying. "Are you sure that's a good idea?"

The woman had just tucked her thumbs into her ever present work belt and shrugged. "It can't hurt. I've already done fucked it all up. And Lenore is an adult now, so it isn't like they can be takin' her from us... I mean from you. Even if we did know where she was."

Then her face took on a pained and earnest expression, "I've got to fix this. Her parents may have some insight as to where she may have run ta." I saw her eyes burn with a dangerous fire when she mentioned Lenny's parents. We hadn't disclosed what we had figured out on our own, but it was plain to see that McGrath had sussed out the abuse and it ignited the Irish temper that burned deep in her hazel eyes, which she controlled so very well.

It was frightening how when she quieted and calmed, it felt like she became the most dangerous person I had ever met. And I loved the woman for it because all that rage was directed to protecting someone we held as precious to us. She had a thing for our curly-haired runner that anyone but Speedy could see.

I smiled involuntarily at the thought of Lenny's curly hair that most woman would die for. She hated it for some unfathomable reason. If I didn't love my straight ebony hair so much, I'd have loved to curl mine like hers. Those lush curls gave her a certain something that made you want to smile at her. Unless of course, you were riding as a passenger when she was driving, then you didn't notice her hair, or anything else, as your life flashed before your eyes.

I had slowly nodded. I didn't like the idea of contacting her parents, knowing what we knew, and we even instructed the agency we hired not to contact them. But we were getting frantic. We just wanted to know that she was ok, she was like my little sister. If we could find her, talk to her, that would be enough even if she decided to stay away. She was family, and we just wanted her to know that.

I said, "Alright, but take the truck, it'll be more convenient."

She opened her pie hole to argue, but I cocked an eyebrow expectantly and assured her, "There are only two correct responses here missy, yes ma'am, or yes Paya." I crossed my arms in a dare. She could squish me in a moment just by flexing one of those muscular arms of hers. Not an unpleasant way to leave this world.

I gave a super toothy grin as she seemed to deflate and capitulate. "Yes, Paya." Then she narrowed her eyes and snarked, "You, Miss Doshi, are just lucky you're so fuckin' cute, or I'd be obligated ta teach ya the folly of pushin' me." I fluttered my eyelashes at her, my grin getting bigger.

She smiled back and rolled her eyes and looked at Ange. "Jaysus, how can ya say no ta that?"

Tabby shook her head and said in a mock-serious tone, "You

can't. I've tried. I failed. She's like a kitten you just want to cuddle. I've found it's just best to let her get her way."

Pleased, I started nodding my head. Then narrowed my eyes at her and asked, "Have you eaten today Tabs? You're looking awfully gaunt."

My best-est friend rolled her copper eyes and then droned out, "Yes Paya." Then she addressed the Irishwoman who was trying hard not to chuckle, "See what I mean? I swear, between her and Teresa, I'm going to blow up like a balloon."

This time, it was Ange who pulled me out of the recent memories. She moved closer to the window and pointed across Flotilla Pier where our service truck pulled into its spot by the storage units. "She's back." She was already in motion, and we went to follow.

I paused just a moment when I saw two other people getting out of the truck with the unmistakeable redhead, then I dashed after the others. "Wait up brats." My mind racing, wondering who McGrath had with her.

Chapter 7 – Siblings

We reached the truck as McGrath reached over to take a heavy looking duffel bag from a cute young woman who looked suspiciously like a slightly younger Lenore. Her flowing curls tumbled over her shoulders and spilled down her back to her waist. I could easily see Speedy letting her's grow out like that, it was pretty spectacular.

The tall and gangly boy that stood beside her was younger but much taller, and I could see the family resemblance. My eyes narrowed, and I felt anger rising from the pit of my stomach as my eyes fastened on the yellowing bruise under his dark brown eyes.

Then my blood ran cold and everything made more sense to me. Lenore had a brother and sister suffering the same abuse she had. Dear lord, she blamed herself. Now the extreme reaction didn't seem so extreme anymore. It wasn't just the shame she felt, thinking it was her fault she got abused, but it was a guilt that probably gnawed at her every day knowing she got out and her siblings didn't.

She probably harbored that guilt, thinking she could have done something more. Didn't she understand that it wasn't her fault nor responsibility? She was just a child at the time.

Now it takes a lot for me to actually hate someone, I don't think I have really truly hated anyone in my life, I'd rather find the good things in people and bring those to the forefront. But I found myself actively hating the people who have broken our girl so completely like that. Her parents would never be able to redeem themselves in my eyes.

I fought back a tear and smiled when they saw us approaching, and the girl moved slightly, interposing herself between her brother and us. She was protecting him from unknown people. I saw Lenny's fire in her eyes.

McGrath, looking haggard and exhausted, moved forward in a similar gesture, giving the siblings a reassuring look. Then she looked back at us and said, "Ladies, let me introduce Lenore's sister Christine Elgin, an' her sprout of a brother, Robert."

She looked almost lovingly at the frightened looking young adults and said, "Kids, this is Miss Paya Doshi, Miss Angie Wells, and..."

The girl sputtered out, her eyes looking about ready to pop out of her head, "Tabby Cat! You didn't tell us this Tabitha lady you spoke of was Tabby Cat, McGrath!"

McGrath chuckled. "I find myself forgettin' that wee fact at times. Yes, Miss Tabitha Romanov, Tabby Cat. These are the women I told ya about. They run the Flotilla Project along with yer sis."

Tabby was all toothy grins. Getting her silly on. She offered a hand to Christine, who shook it with gusto. Robert was more restrained and still hadn't said a word. He shied away from our offered hands. I caught him whispering to his sister, "They're all so pretty." Which made me blush a bit. Compared to the woman

I surrounded myself with, I was chopped liver.

Before I could say anything, McGrath caught each of our eyes before locking gazes with Ange, almost in challenge as she said, "Tina and Bob here are gonna be stayin' with me fer a spell. Just until we find Lenore. Maybe I'll be puttin' them to work on the renovation to let them earn their keep."

The tall Irishwoman shot a wink to the siblings who seemed to huddle closer together like they were lending support to each other. I had seen that before in other children who had floated through the Flotilla from time to time, who came from broken homes of abuse. They only had each other.

I silently thanked God that Nat and Wil were too young to have developed that fear before Stephanie found the Flotilla after her husband wound up doing porridge for almost beating her to death. All those kids knew now was love as they have dozens of loving parents now through the Flotilla and us.

Angie shook her head and countered, "No. They can stay here on the Persephone."

McGrath stilled and reached an arm out to pull the kids close to her, and her Irish accent seemed to thicken as she said tonelessly, "No, they'll be stayin' with me on the Deirdre until we bring Lenore home. I owe her. I owe them." The way she had calmed felt like the ocean in the eye of a hurricane, a false lull that hid the oncoming storm swell that would take out everything in its path.

It would have been sexy as heck if it didn't scare the hell out of me. Angie didn't even flinch.

They maintained eye contact for what seemed like hours but was actually barely the span of two heartbeats before Ange nodded once. McGrath broke into a smile and said, "Lovely." She sort of let it bounce out in three syllables like she had done with Mr. Hastings that first day we met her.

Then she looked at the kids. Christine shivered, even in her coat, as a snowflake landed on her lashes. I looked up, the storm was gaining in intensity as the temperature had dropped noticeably in the last few minutes. Mc Grath said, "Let's get the wee ones inside before they freeze to death out here. We can talk. Christine shared a fascinating tale with me that may tell us where our fuzzy one has gotten herself off too."

I almost blurted, "Of course! And we can get you all fed. You must be starving after the long drive."

The smarmy redhead shared her signature half smirk with the kids, "Told ya. This one's got an odd obsession with feedin' everyone."

All the evil ones present shared a chuckle. I offered an indignant, "Hey!" Then grinned at their continued chuckles. Well fine, maybe I did... but... I looked over at Tabby and suppressed an involuntary shudder. I can never forget how emaciated my best friend had been before June discovered her, living the life of a water gypsy in the floating slums on the river. She even pushed it to the point of passing out from lack of food, rather than asking for help. My friend can be so bloody stubborn and proud at times. I'll never let another person do that to themselves on my watch, ever.

Angie gave a quick verbal tour of the Flotilla as we walked the dock and boarded the Persephone. My mind was working double time. Speedy had a brother and sister. How did we not know this? We were the worst friends ever. Christine had ideas as to where Lenny had gone?

Once we were all in the pilot house and shut out the cold, I shook the snow from my hair and gave everyone a silly grin when I realized they were watching me shake like a dog to shed the frigid flakes.

I said, “Children, sit. I'll order up some food. If you need the loo, it is just through those doors in Lenore's cabin.”

Christine stood taller. “I'm not a child. I'm eighteen, thank you very much.”

I had to smile, and I inclined my head in acceptance. She was so much like her sister.

Both of them kept glancing at the door to Speedy's cabin. I understood. It was where their sister who they haven't seen in two years, lived... well until recently. Robert looked conflicted while Christine looked positively curious. Angie smirked and shook her head, “Go on and take a look. That's Lenore's flat in there.”

The two were off in a shot. And our smiles fell as we turned to McGrath. “Lenny has siblings?”

She nodded slowly and said, “Imagine my shock when I

arrived at the Elgin's to speak with her parents and Christine answered the door. Seems Frizzy had more secrets than just the one. I heard a commotion in the place while a frightened Tina tried sendin' me away, sayin' it was a bad time to have visitors."

Her emotions bled away as that scary calm came back, "I asked if eveythin' was ok in there. Everythin' was becomin' clearer. It was obvious what Lenore was runnin' from, but these new pieces of information were what magnified her reaction ta mahy questions."

She looked up from her hands, her eyes devoid of any emotion, they were like pools of ice. I knew that if this woman ever snapped, there would be violence to spare for whoever that ice gaze was for. "Then I saw Bob, backing inta the livin' room beyond, their Da followin' him, all red faced. The man swayed like a drunk. And I saw the fresh bruise on Bobby's face."

We all turned to Speedy's door at the sound of a young man's voice. Robert was standing in the doorway behind an anxious looking Christine. "She stepped into the house and moved between dad and me, and asked, 'What's goin' on here? I'll be askin' ya to leave the boy alone.' And dad flipped out. He was drunk and mad that I had forgotten to wash the dishes. It was my fault, I shouldn't have forgotten. And here was this buff woman telling him to stop hitting me. I was scared to death for her. She didn't know what he could do."

Christine put an arm around Robert and led him to the conference table, and they sat as she continued for him, smiling with a hint of hero worship at McGrath. “He started on a tirade about how he could discipline his children any way he saw fit and yelled at her to, 'get the fuck out of my house!'. She had just calmly said, 'With pleasure. I'll be takin' the children with me now, ta be with their sister.' Then she placed a hand on Robert's shoulder.”

She said as the rest of us found our seats to listen to the tale, “I was so scared he was going to hurt her, he's been extra angry since someone called the police on him a couple months back. Mum came out of the kitchen as Dad grabbed McGrath's arm to pull it away as he screamed at her, 'No you won't, and you'll get out of here now if you know what's good for you.' He started to raise his fist but paused when he couldn't yank her arm away from Robert.”

Robert shook his head and offered, “I've never seen him hesitate like that. But McGrath said calmly, 'I'll be thankin' ya to remove your hand from mahy arm, lest it be the last thing ya remember in this life. You may be able to bully those ya should be protectin', but let's see what ya can do against someone who can fight back.'”

He said with awe tingeing his voice, “I've never seen dad afraid before until I saw the blood drain from his face after staring at her for a moment, I think he almost pissed his pants. He released her and then she just looked over at mum. 'You can be comin' with us too if ya wish. I'm takin' them to Lenore.'”

Christine chimed in, “Mum is too afraid to leave or say

anything. She pretends she doesn't notice when his anger spills over from her onto us. She says it is just the drink, and that dad is a good man."

She looked down in shame. "She just shook her head. Then McGrath handed her a card and said to her, 'Just call anytime ta speak ta the kids, or if ya need help.' Then she spun on dad and said in that frosty tone again, 'If ya' try ta stop me or ta' call the bobbies, I'll be more than happy ta share with them what I saw. I'm not afraid of ya and would be more than happy ta help puttin' ya behind bars. Do we have an understandin'?'"

Robert shook his head in disbelief. "He... let us go. McGrath was badass."

His smile grew as the Irishwoman blushed. "It wasn't all that. But ya two are safe now."

Christine looked at her accusingly. "You don't understand. Lenore was the only one of us strong and brave enough to try to get out. I stayed for Robert after I turned eighteen."

Robert groused out, "She left us."

His sister countered with venom, "She got out. We weren't her responsibility Bob, she was just a kid like us. She took care of us for so long, and she was just a kid. You need to get rid of the chip on your shoulder and be happy for her."

He shrugged. "But she ran again. We're here, but where is she?"

McGrath interjected like she was talking to small children, "That isn't her fault, it was mine for pushin'. With yer help, we'll find her and bring her home."

She gave a big smile. "And with that, why don'tcha share your tidbit of information with the girls, lass."

I said as I rushed over to the coffee station and put a kettle on, "Hold that thought. Let me get some hot cocoa started for you two, some coffee for the rest of us and get some pizza ordered."

I watched the kids as I ordered up some food and got hot drinks ready to combat the cold outside. This was a dangerous game McGrath was playing. Christine may be an adult, but Robert was a minor. Was what she did akin to kidnapping, even if it were for the sake of the children? I was definitely on her side and the children's on this.

I'd have to get some discreet advice from a lawyer and discuss with Robert if he'd like to be an emancipated minor or have his sister assigned as legal guardian. I'm sure we could get their mother to agree, and maybe get her some help in the process.

Domestic abuse is a terrible thing, the victims usually believe that they are being punished for doing something wrong, that it is their fault. I couldn't bring myself to be angry with the woman. Fear like that can eat away at your soul. And their father sounds as if he abused alcohol on top of everything.

I'm sure the only reason the police aren't knocking on McGrath's door already, is her threat to expose the man. There was an outside witness now, and the wanker had to be sweating bullets. I just hope he doesn't take it out on Lenore's mother.

Once we speak with a lawyer, maybe I can convince McGrath

to file a report anyway, even if it doesn't lead to anything, it will take some pressure off of the mother for a spell. If we can get him out of the house for a bit, maybe we could convince Lenore's mum to leave too, and seek help.

I looked over at the redhead who was listening intently to the kids discussing the trip to the Flotilla with Ange, and what they thought of London. They had only been to London a few times and thought it was amazing. McGrath caught me looking, and she inclined her head slightly, letting me know we were on the same page.

Too many things to think about just then, and I had people to feed.

I handed out hot drinks, and I sat and asked Christine, "So, you have insight as to where we can find your sister?"

Christine looked around as she sipped her hot cocoa and nodded slowly. She put the mug down but kept her hands wrapped around it, letting the heat of the liquid inside warm her. "To tell the truth, I never once thought she was in London. She always spoke of the place she saw as safe, and I really thought she'd been there this whole time. I was going to bring Bobby there when he turned eighteen."

I prompted, seeing a slight glint of mischief in her eyes that reminded me so much of Speedy. The little tease was having fun drawing it out. She took another sip, and I almost exploded in need to know, but my dignity was saved by Angie blurting out, "Oh for the love of god girl, spit it out."

The girl grinned in triumph as she set her cup back down and then exhaled. She said in a distracted voice as she looked out the windows toward the west, "Cardiff. She'll be in Cardiff."

I blinked. Wales? We were right? I asked, "Why Cardiff?"

She blushed, and Robert muttered, "Some Doctor Who bollocks."

She shushed him, "Oh hush Bobby." Then she shrugged and looked around at us. Tabby was unusually quiet, instead of her loquacious self, she was leaning forward with genuine curiosity on her face.

Then the young girl shrugged and said, "It's her safe place. She's a big fan of Doctor Who and especially Captain Jack Harkness. He's... well he's gay like her. Well, he's more pansexual I guess." She looked at her hands then around at us, almost like she were trying not to cringe at some expected backlash.

We all just blinked, it was no surprise to us, and McGrath sat up straighter. That certainly got her attention. I tried hard not to smile. She was so dense just like our Speedy. Everyone saw the attraction between them.

She continued, "She hid that from our parents, dad would have flipped." Then she explained, "In the Torchwood series, Captain Jack made his headquarters in Cardiff. And the city has embraced the shows and seems so inclusive about people with her preferences. She always said that when she got brave enough to run, that's where she was heading."

The reality of that hit hard. To be in a life that you wanted to escape from so badly, that something as simple as shows on the telly influenced you so profoundly with their idyllic message. That need to escape, that survival instinct overriding everything else, driving you.

I looked at the two young people in front of us and could see the same defensive postures, the same caged fear that I recognized from Lenore when she first came to us. I was sure as hell going to bring everything we had to bear to protect them. Not only because it was the right thing to do, but because Lenore was family, that made them family. So please excuse my language here, but nobody fucks with Paya Doshi's family.

I said to the room, trying to keep my voice level, "I'll have the private investigators focus on Cardiff then. If she's there, they'll find her, and we can see about convincing her to come home." I reached my hands across the table and took Robert and Christine's hands and assured them, "We'll find her, and when she learns you're safe now, she'll move hell and high water to be back with you."

Robert sat back and just mumbled, "She left us."

Tabitha finally spoke, after just watching the whole discussion. "Be fair now. She was a child, and she found the strength to get out of a bad situation. She didn't take help from anyone and earned her way into our lives and hearts. She's not the same girl she was, she's stronger now. I can guarantee that she will fight for you if you give her a chance. Your sister is fierce."

She had her copper eyes on his, not blinking, challenging. If you ignored her screwing up her lips to keep blowing an errant lock of her copper hair out of her eyes, she herself looked fierce. I loved my bestie.

Robert broke first and looked away, he started rubbing the side of his hands nervously and nodded. "Ok." The poor boy was blushing now. Tabs has that effect on people.

That's when the runner from Hector's showed up, tapping at the door. The pizza had arrived!

Hector's was a savory new taste that Lenny had introduced us to. Gertrude's was our goto pizza establishment, but she would only deliver on exceedingly rare occasions, and with much bribing. But Speedy showed us the tantalizing culinary delight of Hector's, who does deliver.

She shared that Hector would always bring an extra large pie out to the back alley on Saturday nights for the people living on the streets in his neighborhood. She doesn't think we know that she uses part of her salary to fund a Hector's pizza every night for the people who are invisible to most of society.

I paid Jerry, the delivery guy from the pizzeria, and then brought the pie to the drooling lemmings at the conference table. They were all sitting straight, their eyes on the box. Oooo I had the power! I grinned like a madwoman.

Tabby growled like an enraged kitten. Angie said, "You are a wicked woman, now set it down before we pitch you overboard."

I pursed my lips in a saucy grin then asked, “Oh yeah? You and who's army?” To a one, they all pointed at the muscular Irishwoman who had one eyebrow cocked expectantly at me. I trailed off, “Oh... that army.” I stuck my tongue out at McGrath as I slid the pizza to the middle of the table and opened the lid, to everyone's chuckles.

As I watched them all dig in, my eyes drifted to the younger Elgins as my mind wandered to Speedy. My stomach clenched as I made a silent promise to the universe. We would find her, we would reunite her with her siblings, and we would protect them.

I sat back and smiled as we ate and got to know Speedy's siblings better. The worry gnawing in my gut for our girl relinquishing its death grip on my innards, allowing me to breathe again. Just the low ache of concern for a loved one sat in the back seat while we laughed with our young guests.

I haven't seen McGrath smile once since Lenore ghosted, but here she was laughing and smiling with the group. I had already decided that she was going to be my next project after we reunited Speedy with her. She kept her personal life so far removed from her almost obsessive work life.

We had been slowly breaking through her armor the past couple months, and have gleaned a few things about her life growing up as a master woodworker's daughter. Being close to us with common concerns has made her feel safer to be herself around us.

When I noted that Robert was dozing off in his seat. I sat up straighter and nudged my chin toward him as I said, “That's it for tonight you surly lot. The kids need to rest. We can discuss our plans at the Steinberg tomorrow. And what we're going to do about getting Robert to school.”

I crossed my arms across my chest and arched an eyebrow in a challenge to the group. The adults all droned out, “Yes Paya.” And I grinned hugely, feeling like a pleased chipmunk. See even a McGrath type person is trainable.”

Chapter 8 – Cardiff

Just like every afternoon in recent memory, I was walking along Clarence Embankment beside the River Taff, heading to work at the Blue Dog Pub. It wasn't glamorous work, but it was work and paid for my tiny flat above Mr. and Mrs. Kennison's little garage.

Cardiff wasn't exactly all I had made it out to be in my head. The safe haven and accepting culture that would let me be me without any expectations. I quickened my pace and muttered, "Well except the expectation that you'll be to work on time." I didn't need to be sacked.

I missed my old life at the Flotilla, where I felt like I was helping, contributing to something bigger than myself. Helping people in similar situations to myself. Now I helped grabby men with their drink orders and made sure they have plenty of salted pretzels. But this is just temporary until I can get better situated to find a way to help out those in need here.

I glanced out over the water as I pulled my heavy winter coat tighter around me to fight the frosty air. Then I froze. "Shite!"

My eyes were locked on a familiar green barge moving inland from Cardiff Bay to the little marina on the opposite bank. McGrath? What was she doing here? My heart was thudding in my chest, and I could feel panic rising in me, as well as a familiar longing to see the Amazonian Irishwoman. I growled at myself. She was going to, and probably did, expose me to the women I saw as family, so why did I still harbor this bloody attraction to her?

I hustled along, distracted by the shamrock-colored vessel in the distance. Then I realized the most likely reason for her to be in Cardiff and exhaled a breath I hadn't even realized I was holding. If she was here, that meant the Steinberg renovation was done. She'd never leave the job unfinished.

That meant she was likely heading to Ireland to see her Nana and keep her promise. Cardiff was a convenient stop to wait out that huge winter storm that was rolling in, that's all. The Celtic Sea and Saint George's Channel were already getting choppy according to the alerts I read on my cheap pay as you go mobile this morning.

With one last longing look at the Deirdre as she pulled into port, I turned back to the lane and hurried along. Killian was not a pleasant man to work for, but he was fair, paid a fair wage, and the tips were good. I didn't need him sacking me over being late for the third time this week. What I wouldn't give for a vehicle of my own.

Heh, who would have thought I'd miss driving. What with the plethora of bad drivers out there and all. I pushed away the flood of unwanted memories of the Flotilla that came washing over me. They were better off without me. Without someone who lied to them every day.

I put in my earbuds and cued up some music on my mobile and cranked up the tunes to take my mind off yet another family I missed so much. One day, I would find my home and make a family that I could keep. I thought I had done that once, but like everything in this cruel world of ours, it was only fleeting.

I arrived to work with a minute to spare and looked back toward the Taff as I held the back door open, before heading inside. I absently wished Hunter safe travels to Ireland, and a happy life, even if she was the most aggravating person on the planet. I felt as if we had connected before she dropped her bomb on me.

The gruff old Welshman gave a sarcastic sounding grunt and quipped, "Would you look at that, will miracles never cease? It seems you actually CAN tell time Gwen."

I shook my head at him as I tied the blue apron around my waist. "If I didn't need this job, I'd be telling you where you can shove your smartassery about now, Killian."

The old man chuckled as he rubbed his grizzled grey beard. He said, "There's the spirit. Now get yer arse to the front, Nancy quit."

I paused and looked up to the heavens. Shite, we were already understaffed. I've seen four barmaids quit in the few weeks I have been here. It takes a rare constitution to put up with the raucous and lewd behavior of the men who frequented a Welsh pub. Most women won't put up with the immature behavior and unwanted advances. I've suffered far worse and survived, so it didn't bother me as much as most. I was a survivor. That's all I did... survive.

I absently wondered how the Steinberg had turned out. I had put a lot of work I was proud of into it and was sure it turned out beautifully if Hunter had anything to say about it.

I adjusted my nametag which read Gwen, on my chest and steeled myself to go out into the battleground that was the Blue Dog. I had taken to going by my middle name when I arrived in Cardiff. Guinevere. I figured I was remaking myself for the second time in my life, may as well start with a clean slate. Plus my British ID showed me as Lenore Guinevere Statham, and I didn't want to start from scratch again.

I put on my practiced fake smile and pushed my way through the door and into the noisy bar. I grabbed a regular's hand as he went to grab my waist, and pushed him away. “You're cut off Louie.”

The man said in a slur, “But Gwen, I love you.”

I stepped up to the bar and took a tray Killian was holding out for me as I said, “I love you too Louie, but your wife says there's no room in your house for me. Pay your tab and go sober up, you know the rules, no touching.”

The heavyset man placed both hands over his heart and hung his head like a puppy. “If I must.”

Killian said in his gruff tones, “Oh you must, you lush.” Then to me, he said, “Table three.” I nodded as I took the tray and he boomed out, “Bailey, take your break.”

Oh for fuck's sake, I'd have the entire pub until she got back. The pleasantly plump, petite woman sashayed and twisted through the pub toward the back, her long black locks trailing. I sighed, yet another woman who didn't have to battle the curse that was my hair. At least I had it in a tight-ish ponytail today.

She reveled in all the attention. She gave me a little wink as she passed by, handing me her tickets. "Back in a flash hon." I had to smile at her, she was such a sweetie. Of all the people in the world, she sort of reminded me of Angie's Stephanie.

The next nine hours were excruciating, I was on a double shift to pick up more lolly, and also to stay in Killian's good graces, and still had three hours to go. I wondered if it were possible to die from boredom, just repeating the same thing over and over ad nauseam. I really needed to find something different. You can only serve so many trays of beer and spirits before your brain falls out onto the floor to be kicked around by people heading to the bar. Plop, squish.

The winter storm had hit, and that made more people pack into the pub to stay out of the biting cold. The wind was whipping the snow around.

It wasn't the wet fluffy flakes which just seem to remind you of sledding as a child, but those smaller, dry flakes that seem to not want to stick to each other and just blow around like a gossamer fog with every punishing gust of wind. And they seem to find every vulnerability in your clothing to chill you and remind you why winter can sometimes be a right wanker at times.

Speaking of wankers, I turned toward the heavyset man in the bright, heavy clothing of a dockworker. I interposed my empty tray I was bringing up to Killian to put in a drink order for table six, between myself and the man who had groped my arse, causing him to let go.

I said to the man, “You're cut off sir. Pay your tab and be on your way.” He stood up and moved closer, getting into my personal space, I pulled the tray closer to my chest. For the most part, the boisterous men who frequent the pub were a good lot. But when someone who wasn't a regular toed the line of the rules, it made me nervous, as most men are bigger than me.

I'm pretty sure that's why Killian has helped enforce my self-made rule that any involved in unwanted touching or groping has to pay their tab and head out. I think some of the regulars do it when they are ready to leave just to be smart arses.

This guy, I didn't know. I glanced at the bar as the man started to speak, and was relieved to see old man Killian watching intently. “Come on darlin' why you gotta be like that?” His harsh accent had a rough eastern European flair to it, and that matched his appearance with his stubble hair and beard.

He blocked my retreat to the bar, and I was suddenly aware of just how much bigger than me he was. I said, keeping the waver out of my voice, but feeling a little better as I saw some of the pub regulars taking note of things and their expressions becoming dourer, “House rules. Hands off the staff.” Well, my house rule anyway.

He reached out a huge paw of a hand that looked cracked and calloused from years of hard physical labor as he said, “Come now, there's no need to..."

He stopped mid-sentence when a hand grabbed his arm, stopping him from touching me again. A body moved between the dockworker and me, causing me to take a step back.

I think my heart stopped beating and I froze in a combination of panic and overwhelming relief as I gazed upon McGrath, with the most dangerous look I had ever seen on her face as she said with a tone of a star being frozen over as its energy is stripped violently from it, "I wonder."

The man's face changed from one of lasciviousness to a seething hate as he tried to yank his arm free of her grasp, I think he was a little startled when his arm didn't budge, and I saw her tighten her grip. Those hands that could create something out of nothing. Years of carving and construction honing the muscles and sinuous tendons in her hands into steel bands. The man winced a bit, and I saw a shadow of doubt fogging that rage on his face as he asked, "Wonder what?"

She said in that same emotionless tone that fired off every trigger in my body, screaming that she was an apex predator on the hunt, "I wonder how many doctors it's gonna be takin' to extract this barstool from yer arse, ya gobshite."

The dockworker and I both followed her eyes down to her other hand. She was holding one of the industrial steel barstools in her hand like it was of no more consequence than holding a cricket bat. It must have weighed eight or nine kilos. She added, "The lady told ya ta pay up and be on yer way."

The man's anger gave way to fear as he stared at the stool as she tightened her grip on the metal tubing. Killian had arrived and tossed his towel over his shoulder. "Is there a problem here?"

The man tried to pull his arm back again, and she didn't let go as she said in her Tweedledee accent, "No, not at all. This nice man was about ta pay his tab and be along his way, now wern'tcha?" She gave a smile that sent chills down my spine.

The man nodded, and she let go of his arm and sat the stool down with a clank and slid onto it in the middle of the floor as the guy rubbed his arm and said, "No. No problem. I was just leavin' anyway."

McGrath smiled at the man and said, "Lovely."

The guy threw some bills on the table and stepped wide around us and scurried through the door. Then the pub erupted into a cheer as all the Welshmen hoisted their mugs and took a deep pull.

Now that my initial shock had dissipated, I gaped at the redheaded Irishwoman, my fear, and anger surfacing. How could I be so unlucky as to have the woman who was the bane of my existence pick this pub to get a drink in on her way to Ireland? Had I wronged the gods in some manner that made them want to punish me this way?

I croaked out, "Hunter? What are you doing here?" Even I could hear the waver in my voice. I hated her so much because there was an odd tinge of hope in my tone.

She furrowed her brows as if I had spoken in an alien

language. She tilted her head, gave me that infuriating cocky smirk of hers and said as she shrugged, “Isn't it obvious, Lenore? I've come ta take ya home.”

Chapter 9 – Reunited

We stood in the blowing snow in the halo of light that spilled into the alleyway from the fixture above the door. I shivered in the cold, being too daft to have brought my coat with me when I dragged her out through the kitchen and into the alley. I spun on her and asked again, this time, my anger and fear bolstered my voice as I repeated, "What are you doing here McGrath?"

She smirked. "So it's McGrath again, now is it?"

So many emotions were boiling over inside me, pushing away the cold. I couldn't sort them all out, and some didn't even make sense to me. I started into her. "What gives you the right? What gives you the right to destroy my life, then presume that you can come in like a knight on a white horse to rescue me?"

I felt anger and shame that shook me as violently as the cold had a just a moment ago, "I was happy, finally happy. Now it's all gone."

I sucked in a quick breath and steeled myself. "And I can take care of myself, I don't need a bloody Amazonian leprechaun to chase away the likes of that wanker. I'm stronger now, I can take care of myself!"

I wiped the tears that were flowing down my cheeks, leaving icy trails in the blowing wind, as the snow swirled around us like the promise of new anguish to be had. I started to shake, aborting sobs as I whispered, "I was finally happy."

I opened my mouth to continue my tirade, suddenly bolstered

with all the emotion and confusion I felt for this Irishwoman, who I haven't been able to get off my mind since that Saturday she had shared private things with me about her past. How dare she make me like her.

The woman looked frustrated, good, it was good to see that the mighty McGrath could be shaken. I started to hiss out, “How dare...”

And she interrupted, “For the love of God, Lenore. Shut yer fecking trap fer just one moment wouldja?” And then her lips were on mine, and I froze. All those emotions that were warring inside me surged back to the surface as I tried to sort through them. McGrath was kissing me?

I hated her didn't I? McGrath was kissing me.

Why did I want nothing but this? Hunter was kissing me.

As my mind fogged over, one thought washed through me, warming me, making my entire being buzz as I curled my toes in my shoes... Hunter.

I found my traitorous body responding as if it had a will of its own. And it wanted McGrath more than anything else in this world. More than food, more than breathing. Had I... had I been wrong about her? Oh shut the hell up Lenore, Hunter is kissing you! I melted into her and cried as I kissed back, eagerly. I drank her in like a woman dying of thirst in a burning desert who had just stumbled upon an oasis.

The sexiest woman I had ever met was expressing her feelings for me though our desperate kiss, causing my legs to turn to jelly.

I thought she disliked me, that she was annoyed by my presence, so had made it her job to make my life a living hell. I grudgingly found that I had a huge amount of respect for her, which made me even more infuriated with her.

How could someone be so blessed with looks, character, and ethics, while being so smug and annoying? How was it fair to the rest of us who were unsure of our own moral core, and who felt like we'd look better with a sack over our heads?

I smiled into the kiss. Who the hell cared? Hunter was kissing me. She smiled when she felt my smile on her lips and then pulled away, leaving me gasping for air. I'm sure I would have happily perished from lack of oxygen if she would have just kept kissing me. Her lips had been so soft and powerful all in the same instant, just like her.

She had her smarmy half smirk back on her lips as she ran her hands up through my ponytail and pulled my scrunchy off to let my hair spill down around my shoulders. She said as that smirk turned into a cocky, toothy grin, "There now. Are ya ready ta listen now?"

I bit my lower lip as I stared at hers, glistening in the dim light in the alley. I glanced up into her intense hazel eyes and nodded bashfully. I don't think I could have figured out just how to speak just then. Every nerve was buzzing with excitement. I nodded dumbly again as she wiped the tears from my cheeks with her thumbs. Unlike the rest of her soft skin, her hands were rough and calloused from years of working with wood. They were so...

McGrath.

She lost her cocky smirk and then her eyes softened as she said with a tone I had never heard from her, a tone that set something inside of my gut ablaze with need, “I've come ta take ya home, Len.”

I shook my head slowly. “You don't understand.”

She stopped me. “I understand more than ya know. All the people who love ya are worried sick. An what am I ta tell Christine and Bobby if I come home empty handed?”

I went stock still at that, and the cold air around me started to bite again as I realized I was freezing. I looked up at her, almost pleading. “Christine and Robert?”

She gave a toothy grin at that and said, “Of course. They're waitin' on the Deirdre at the marina on the River Taff.”

I covered my mouth when tears blurred my vision again, I gave her a pleading look, begging her to tell me she wasn't playing with me and my emotions. My brother and sister were really here? They got out too? She softened and nodded once. I started to reach up and paused. I had to fight that urge to reach my hand up and run it through her silky pixie cut, to feel the tickling stubble of the shaved portions of her head. She had brought my family with her?

Then softer than I have ever heard her speak, she nudged her chin toward the door and prompted, “Come now. Get yer coat before ya freeze to death out here, and let's get ya back to where ya belong.” She paused a moment before smirking and adding,

"Frizzy."

I couldn't stop the smile that threatened to split my face as I backhanded her lightly in the stomach. I almost purred when I hit a wall of solid muscle which I had to admit was sexy as hell. Then I hesitated and looked down at my hands as I pressed them hesitantly on her stomach and asked, "Why... why did you kiss me, Hunter?"

A finger on my chin guided my eyes up across her freckled strewn face to meet those hazel eyes that burned with so many emotions. She said in all earnestness, "Isn't it obvious? I forgot how ta smile when me Da left me. But then I met you, and now... now you are my smile, Lenore."

Oh dear lord in heaven, I melted on the spot, and she smiled down at me and bent down to capture my lips with hers in a whispering kiss. She pulled away, leaving me wondering if it were possible to freeze to death while simultaneously being burned alive from the heat gathering inside my core.

I must have had a goofy look on my face as I just stood there, because her smarmy smirk was back as she nudged her chin toward the door. Oh! I started moving, who was I to say no to an infuriating Amazon who had just kissed me... twice? I obediently started for the door then squeaked when she slapped my arse playfully, "There's mahy girl."

I hustled in, took off my apron, and grabbed my coat before heading out into the pub. Killian looked up from the bar and narrowed his eyes as I approached. Some sort of realization crossed his face, and he seemed to soften a bit as I reached him. He said in his thick Welsh accent, "So that's it now is it?"

I nodded and screwed my face up in apology, handed him the apron, and stood up on my tiptoes to kiss his cheek. "I'm sorry," I whispered as I pulled way and started back toward the back.

"Hey, Gwen."

I turned back to look at him as he said with a little smile, "Your hair looks good down like that."

I blushed a little and gave him a pathetic little wave. "Bye, Killian, thanks for everything."

He winked at me, and I exhaled and turned back to the kitchen door, paused to steeled myself, then stepped trough. I slipped into my coat and stepped into the alley.

I thought I caught a ghost of worry shadowing the Irishwoman's face as I stepped out. It washed away into her usual self-assured cockiness as she gave a crooked smile and reached out a hand. I tried not to smile, honest I did, but I failed as I pushed back my unruly curls from my face and bashfully took her strong, calloused hand that felt like a furnace in mine.

She said as we started walking, "Come on then, the world can't wait around fer ya, Frizzy."

I huffed then growled, "Watch it or you'll be the next face featured on a milk carton."

She chuckled, and I shook my head as I asked, "Why do you go from sweet to poisonous in the fives seconds flat?"

She cocked her head and looked down at me with mischief

twinkling in her eyes as we rounded the end of the alley and onto the walk. “Because I've never met anyone as scrappy as you who can take it and dish it right back at me. You don't allow me to take mahyself too seriously, and call me on mahy bullshite. What d'ya think drew me to ya?”

I felt as if I had been doing an inordinate amount of blushing the past few minutes. I felt a new heat feathering across my cheeks and down my neck. I muttered with a wry grin, “Well if you weren't such a bloody wanker all the time I wouldn't have to call you on it.”

Her smile became a fierce grin as she challenged, “Where would the fun be in that now?” Then she pulled me by the hand closer to her, and she let go of my hand and instead wrapped her arm around my shoulders and hugged me to her as we walked.

She kissed the top of my head and said, “I really did miss ya, Lenore. You had us all scared.”

I just nodded and basked in the warmth radiating off of her as we walked. Then admitted something I would have never thought possible, but the truth rang in my voice as I said in an exhalation, “I missed you too. Even if you are a right pain in my arse.” My smile bloomed at her explosive bout of laughter.

My mind was still swimming with everything that was happening. McGrath had kissed me... and I more than liked it. Hunter was here... to get me. McGrath had kissed me. She brought my brother and sister somehow. Hunter had kissed me. Apparently, Angie and Paya weren't mad at me? I knew sod all about what was up or down just then because I realized just how much I wanted the smarmy, self-righteous, egotistical, pretty, strong, and sexy as hell Irishwoman.

I asked as a gust of wind drove the crystalized snow around us and into our faces, “Where's your vehicle? It's freezing out here. I'll drive.”

She blurted on reflex, “No!” Then lowered her voice and let her Tweedledee accent come out to play, “There'll be no need ta be threatenin' the universe with yer drivin' now. I walked here don'tcha know?”

I stopped walking, pulling her to a stop and looked up at her incredulously. “The marina is a couple kilometers away you warped leprechaun! You expect us to walk in this storm?”

She looked down at me and said, “Now listen, Fuzzy. I've come all this way ta bring you home, ya wee daft woman. Don't be expectin' me ta pay fer a ride as well.”

I shook my head at her in exasperation,. “You're impossible.” Then I jabbed a finger at her before she could respond. “And no, that's not a compliment you demented shamrock surfer.”

I doubt her grin could have gotten any bigger. Then she surprised me and dipped her head to capture my lips again. Heat rushed through me as I leaned into it as her tongue traced my lips and I gave her access. I wanted her to devour me.

She pulled back with a smirk, satisfied that she had shut me up, “I'll keep ya warm on the walk.” I nodded. Yes, please. She pulled me closer to her and started us toward the bridge to cross the River Taff.

She said offhandedly, “Just so you know, that'd be three kisses now, so I'll be stakin' my claim on ya now.”

I was still in a happy fog and just nodded into her side as I bit my lower lip in need. Just about then I'd let this Amazon do anything she wanted. Then she added, “Fuzzy,” just to throw a bucket of cold water on my arousal.

I growled and lashed my leg back behind me to kick her arse, then almost fell on my face when she returned it, but she held me firmly so I didn't stumble.

I smiled, feeling as though things were back to normal with us. I asked with a touch of shame in my voice. “How are Ange and Paya? Is the Steinberg done?”

She shrugged. “Angie is worried out of her gourd. Pretty sure she thinks you are her little sister. Paya is Paya, all take charge and criminally cute. She doesn't think we know how much your absence is stressin' her, so Tabby is hangin' around a lot more to keep her mind off you.”

I mumbled, “Sorry.”

She squished me tighter to her for a moment then said, “The Steinberg opens in a week. Yer siblings are hard workers. After we located you, the ladies sent me to come fetch ya. We have to raise anchor as soon as this storm lifts, I still have one task to complete before the openin' ceremony.”

I almost whispered as I cuddled into her side, taking in that scent of sawdust, grease, and soap I had missed so much, “Are

Christine and Robert..."

She nodded. "They're just fine. Robert is a wee bit out of sorts, but he'll come around. And he is a wonder at finishin' the woodwork in the Steinberg. He has a talent." I smiled at that. Bobby always did pick up on things quickly.

She got me to talking about my trek to Watford until I moved on to Cardiff. She didn't seem surprised at all when I confided that it was my original destination when I had originally run away but wound up stuck in London.

I almost asked how they knew where to look, but then in a flash of insight I got it. Christine. She knew me better than anyone. She was my sis. The little rat ratted me out. I smiled, I'd have to thank her.

Then I got almost giddy. Christine and Bob were here! I had missed them so much. It was like a guilty hole in my heart, eating at me everyday. It feels like I had abandoned them in another lifetime. This was my third life now, and I was going to be reunited with them. At that thought, I started to feel apprehensive and frightened. What if they couldn't forgive me for abandoning them?

As if she could read me like an open book, Hunter said softly, "It'll be fine. You'll see." Then she gave me a smirk and said, "And if they push you overboard instead, just think of it as a burial at sea. Easy peasy."

I narrowed my eyes playfully at her and muttered in a petulant tone, "Oh how I loathe thee, let me count the ways."

She was beyond pleased at getting a rise out of me and got some extra bounce in her step as she said, "Well that'll be a problem for ya, seein' as how I'm overly fond of ya. Even if ya only come up ta mahy waist."

I slugged her gut lightly. "I'm not that short."

She nodded. "Says you."

I felt oddly playful and said as I hopped onto my toes as we walked to give her a peck on the lips, "Yeah, says me. Any arguments?"

She was in rare form as she shook her head. "None from up here." Her little barbs at one time would have incensed me, now I almost craved them. Just what had happened to change it? I looked up to her, the wind ruffled her silky pixie cut, and her ears were red with the cold. The confident look on her face as she stared forward made her seem larger than life to me. Oh, ok, Hunter happened.

I snuggled in, and she tightened her grip as we trudged through the blowing snow. Halos of light formed around the streetlights and the lights from the buildings along the lane. It was almost pretty in an urban fairytale sort of way. I sighed into the tall heat generator beside me, realizing the odd feeling bubbling up from deep inside me was my happiness returning with every stride.

We made the last leg of our trek in a comfortable silence, the Deirdre looming closer on the river as we approached the little marina. I swallowed when I saw figures moving in the lights in the windows of the barge. That'd be my estranged siblings.

We walked to the end of the long dock where various pleasure or fishing vessels were moored. I almost chuckled at the banners fluttering in the wind on the green boat. McGrath Handyman Service. I almost chuckled in memory of the first time I had spied the boat in the shadow of the Hammersmith all those months ago. Had it really been nine months now?

The only sound I could hear over the gusting wind was the generator on the boat supplying the heat and lights to the cabin.

The redhead released my shoulder and stepped across the small gap between the dock and the railing of the Deirdre. Then she hopped down onto her deck and held her hands out to me to help me across. I rolled my eyes and groused at her, "I'm not an invalid, woman." Then I stretched out a hand and placed it on the railing then vaulted to the deck of the boat and promptly slipped on the snow and landed on my arse.

Hunter looked down at me, sprawled out on the deck like a wayward crab and covered her mouth with a hand to hide her smile. I growled at her, and she shook her head and offered a hand. I grudgingly took it, and she pulled me to my feet. "Smooth," she said as she walked away toward the main cabin door.

I warned in a pout, "I will end you."

She turned back and winked and said in a deeper, almost sultry tone, "I wouldn't have it any other way."

Eeep. I had to stop myself from biting my lip in want again.

She knocked on the door as she opened it, saying in a singsong voice, "Hello in the cabin."

We stepped down into that marvelously carved space. It was just as awe-inspiring this second time. I froze as I saw the two young people standing up from the table as McGrath moved beside me.

Christine had grown so much, not as much as Bobby, but she looked like a younger me in many ways. Except her curly hair was so beautiful and flowing compared to mine which had a mind of its own.

She stood there a moment, a hand covering her mouth, her eyes seeking and brimming with tears. Bobby crossed his arms over his chest defensively. It was the same posture he got whenever our father got home from a drinking binge. He had an obstinate glare on his face. I could start to see the man he would become as his face had lost so much of its baby fat now as he started to mature.

I took a step forward and opened my arms in an almost pleading gesture. That's all it took and Christine was darting forward to engulf me in a tight hug as she almost sobbed out, "Lenore."

Tears were flowing freely down my face as I tried not to sob as I held my sister for the first time in years. I whispered into her hair, "Peanut. I'm so sorry."

She nodded into my shoulder and pulled back and cocked her head as she examined me. "You... you've changed. You've grown up. There's fire in your eyes now, confidence."

I shrugged and then ran my hands along the sides of her face, pressing her hair down. "You got big. I'm so sorry I left. I just... I couldn't."

She shook her head and gave a smile and hugged me again then stepped aside as I looked over at Bobby, almost pleadingly. She nudged her eyes toward him, and I nodded once at her. I squeezed her shoulder with a hand and stepped around the table. She slid next to Hunter who wrapped an arm around her shoulder.

I stood in front of my brother who had a stubborn look on his face, his arms still crossed across his chest. I straightened the hem of my jacket and said self-consciously, "Hello Bobby."

His first words to me were what I feared, an acrid accusation, "You left us. Abandoned us to... him."

I nodded as my tears started up again. "I did. And I'm so sorry."

We just stood like that, and I said in a small voice, "I missed you so very much Sprout."

We took each other's measure, and I opened my arms in question as I shot him a pleading look. I exhaled in relief as he started nodding as his own tears started to fall and said to me in a cracking voice, "I'm still mad at you."

I nodded in earnest as he hugged me, pulling my feet off the ground. The little sprout had gotten so strong. I sobbed into his shoulder as he gently swayed me from side to side. Then he set me down, wiped his tears with his sleeve like he was embarrassed by them, and then said as he looked over the others, “McGrath got us out of there. Mum is getting help now and 'he' is in a lot of legal trouble now that she is talking. The barrister is trying to get him rehab instead of jail time.”

With my hands on his upper arms, I held him at arm's length, looking him over from head to toe, then ruffled his mop of brown hair. “You need a haircut.” He smirked at that. Oh good god, no... it looked like McGrath's smirk. She was infecting my siblings with a case of the Hunters. I grinned back.

Then McGrath spoke, “What say we catch up over supper and then hit the rack, we raise anchor at first light.”

The two youths said in unison, “Aye aye captain.” She didn't make them call her captain, did she? I cocked and eyebrow at the smug woman, and she winked back.

Then she prompted, “It's yer turn to choose, Bobby. What'll it be tonight?”

He glanced at his sister and asked, “A fryup?” Then he scrunched his head to his shoulders and looked at us in embarrassment. “Breakfast for supper sounds good.”

My stomach gurgled, and everyone chuckled at me as I defended, “I haven't had a bite since breakfast, the pub was slammed today.”

Christine moved over to the kitchen area and started pulling out food from the fridge and a large cast iron pan. I started toward her to help, and she waved me off, growling like me, “Out of my kitchen. Go sit down and warm up, I'll have supper ready in two shakes."

I blinked and opened my mouth to protest, but Hunter moved beside me, lowered her lips to my ear and said softly, with her hot breath sending a thrill down my spine, "It's best ta listen ta her. She didn't take ta mahy diet of canned goods and carry out. So she took over mahy boat. I can't remember the last time there was fresh food, let alone home cooked food on the Deirdre. Now it's everywhere."

Christine pointed at us with the pan then toward the sitting area where a nice little fire was burning in the wood stove. Hunter grinned and said playfully, "Ta tell the truth, I'm a little scared of her."

My sister clucked out as she fired up the stovetop. "Because you have good sense."

My redhead confided only half-jokingly, "I don't know if I'm taking care of her or her me."

I glanced over at Robert as he sat across from us in an overstuffed chair which had hand carved legs. He shrugged and said, "Don't look at me. I know when to keep my mouth shut."

I exhaled in a resigned sigh and then suddenly didn't care as a warm arm wrapped around me and slid me closer on the couch to Hunter. I timidly placed my hands on her upper chest then laid my head on her. She tilted her head to rest on top of mine, and I sighed for a completely different reason then.

I discreetly inhaled her scent and found it soothing and relaxing as well as a little arousing.

We all chatted as my little sis filled the cabin with mouth-watering aromas. It seems there was a short-lived legal battle after McGrath took my siblings away. That's when Mum actually stepped forward and signed the paperwork to make Hunter Robert's temporary legal guardian.

They shared that if I would have them, the NSPCC would prefer a blood relative for permanent guardianship until he turned eighteen. The look of hope they gave me broke my heart that they were worried I wouldn't agree. I blurted out, “Of course! But I'll need to find a flat, my cabin on the Persephone is tiny for three people.”

The looks of relief on my siblings stung a bit, but I understood, I had abandoned them once before.

Hunter knocked me out of licking my wounds as she said hopefully, “Nonsense, there's plenty of room on the Deirdre.” I blinked at her as I rolled through all the ramifications of that statement. She was sure enough that I'd come around to not suffocating her in her sleep to make the offer?

A small part of my brain was wondering how packed it would be in her father's room for us three three Elgins. Or... I blushed. Or would I be staying with Hunter in her room? Then I craned my head and narrowed my eyes up at her. She was being awfully presumptuous, I should just...

She leaned down and kissed me, taking me completely by surprise and causing Bobby to blush and look away as I heard from the kitchen area a dreamy. “Awwww.”

She pulled back, leaving my lips slightly parted in want as I blinked the happy fog away. Then I looked at her accusingly. She defended, "Preemptive strike. You had the chew nails and spit fire look about ya. Ya know, the one where the side of your eyes twitch when you're about ta explain why I'm being presumptuous and all? I claim girlfriend privilege since I struck a proper claim earlier tonight, with Cardiff as mahy witness."

I opened my mouth to speak, but she added, "I'm sure it would hold in a court of law. It's right there, plain as day in the datin' handbook."

My traitorous sister chimed in, "She's right. Now come on everyone. Breafast-y supper is served."

I exhaled in defeat. They were ganging up on me. Then smiled and said as I stood slowly, edging toward the great carved table. "I'll think about it."

Then Hunter realized what I was doing and started to rise quickly as I scurried off toward the table and the food that was setting of the Pavlovian drool response in me. I can't remember the last time I had a home cooked meal. But no matter how fast we were, Bobby had somehow beat us all to a seat and was already dishing his plate high with ham, eggs, and hash browns.

I cocked an eyebrow, and McGrath supplied as she held my seat for me, an act that made me swoon a bit. "I've come ta learn it's a superpower of all teenaged boys."

I nodded in understanding and replied succinctly, "Ah." We all chuckled as Christine joined us.

Bobby said, “Oh shut up and leave me to eat.”

His fork was halfway to his mouth, and I was reaching for the larger bowl of eggs when Hunter cleared her throat. Bobby froze then lowered his fork to his plate with a tired sigh. Then he reached out to take Christine's hand, Hunter took her other and reached a hand to me. I blinked and took it.

I asked incredulously, my eyes a little wide, “You make them say grace? I didn't know you were religious.”

She shrugged at me, more than a little embarrassed as she said, “I'm not so much, but I don't know the first thing about raisin a teenager right, and Christine said yer family is Christian, so I figure it's the right thing ta do?”

I blinked at her. She was awkward as hell, but I could see that determination in her to do her best for them, whether they wanted it or not. This was the quintessential McGrath, the drive to do the right thing whether you wanted it or not.

Christine started, “We tried to tell her that we don't...” She trailed off at the cocked eyebrow on Hunter's face. She lowered her head and said, “Yes ma'am.”

The Irishwoman grinned like a loon then lowered her head, Bobby followed suit so I did as well. I got a little squeeze of my hand as a reward, and I tried not to smile as she stumbled through a makeshift prayer, “Lord. We'll be thankin' ya fer bringin' us all together. Oh, and fer the food and stuff. And fer takin' care of our loved ones.” She let go of my hand but then grabbed it again before I could pull my hand away, and she added, “Oh, and...

amen."

She released our hands, and we all looked up. The look Christine had on her face was priceless. She was grinning at McGrath like you would a puppy who was trying hard to jump up onto the furniture and we all said, "Amen," just as awkwardly as McGrath had.

I patted my girl's hand reassuringly. Whoah, I have a girl. One I want to strangle half the time, but still, I had a girl. "That was lovely, Hunter." I strung out lovely like she did.

Then I froze when she sighed and cringed. Right on cue, before I could ask about her reaction, Christine was asking with bright eyes, "Your name is Hunter?"

I muttered, "Bloody hell." Then squinted one eye as I looked sheepishly at the redhead glaring down at me. "Ummm... sorry?"

She muttered as she reached over to snag a slice of toast and violently tear a bite off, "Oh you'll be sorry you frizzy-haired Judas." She gave a grin that promised an eternity of teasing.

Then she said like a school teacher explaining something to a small child, "Mahy name is McGrath, thank you very much. You best remember it."

My sister nodded seriously as she ate and said without missing a beat, "Yes Hunter."

My girl sputtered out to Robert, "Dear Lord in heaven save us all, now there's two of 'em."

My traitorous brother just nodded seriously and said around a mouthful of potatoes, "Yes, McGrath."

Hunter shot him her signature smirk. “There's a boy.”

With that, he shot both Christine and I a McGrath worthy smirk. The little suck up! My sis confirmed my exact thoughts by saying, “Suck up.” We all had a good chuckle, then I paused as I ate to look around.

This was all such a surrealistic dream. My brother and sister were here with me, they got out. I glanced over at the impossible Irishwoman beside me. She had got them out. And she apparently hadn't betrayed me. She had... feelings for me? I sighed and kept eating as we started discussing the years we were apart and what was new in their lives.

They were more excited about the Steinberg than escaping our dad. They found that they loved working with their hands like I did, and had an odd sort of pride in building something for others. McGrath reminded us all that our work would stand in the building long after we were all gone.

That was something to think about. She had a different perspective about these things than anyone I had ever met, and she was constantly making me pause to think. Just chalk it up to another reason I heated up whenever she turned her intense hazels on me.

When supper was over, Robert and I all helped Christine clean up while McGrath went to check on the fuel for the generator. This gave my sis a chance to whisper to me, “She's over the moon for you sis.”

I smiled in the direction the woman had gone and confided,

"When I don't want to wrap her in black plastic and dump the remains in the sea, I'm pretty much head over heels for her too, Peanut."

She didn't miss a beat, always so fast with the comebacks even when we were little kids. "And have you seen that arse?"

I nodded with a dreamy smile on my face, then froze and cocked an eyebrow at her in question. She chuckled at me and slapped my shoulder lightly, "Hey, even us straight girls can appreciate sexy."

So I teased back, "Mine."

She nodded with a wink. "Apparently."

Robert put the last plate into the cabinet as he rolled his eyes, "Just kill me now." He was such a boy.

We all chuckled, and Hunter stepped back in, wiping her hands on a rag. "What did I miss?"

Bobby opened his pie hole, "Just the discussion about your arse."

My girl got her smarmy smirk on and said, "Ay yes, the fine arts." I threw the dishtowel at her as she gave a silly grin and sidestepped it.

Then she looked around and said as she stoked the fire, "Lights out in twenty. Best be off ta bed now."

Bobby gave her a hug and Christine skipped over and said as she gave us each a hug, "Night McGrath, night sis."

I smiled and said, "Goodnight you two."

Then I timidly took Hunter's hand and started following them.

She pulled me to a stop. “Where are ya goin' now?”

I furrowed my brow, oh dear lord, I was presuming too much. I assumed... I mean I didn't expect to sleep together but that we'd share a room. I mean I'd be on the floor or something... I more asked than said, “Your room?”

She nudged her chin to the kids as the went out to the hall. Then she said, “We're in the master suite. They're down the hall. Christine has my old room, and I fixed up the storage hold under the pilothouse inta a cabin for Robert. Teenagers need their own space I'm told.”

Oh. I searched her face, seeing the shadow I expected to see. She was overcoming her own fears by finally accepting her father's quarters for her own, all to give my brother and sister rooms of their own in her home?

She nudged my hip with hers. “Stop overthinkin' and overanalyzin', Frizzy.”

I pursed my lips in frustration then ground out, “When you stop being infuriating.”

She chuckled and grabbed both of my hands and walked backward, dragging me along with a half smile on her lips, “It seems we have a stalemate then.”

I nodded, a playful smile playing at my lips as I stared at hers, mesmerized by them. “Apparently.”

She backed into her father's cabin... no, her cabin and then released my hands. I exhaled. Then started babbling nervously, “I'll just need a blanket and pillow and can sleep in that chair there. I'll need to get to my flat before we leave in the morning to get my things and let the Kennison's know I'll not be back. I can..."

She blurted out, "Dear Lord woman, would ya shut yer yap fer just a moment?" Then her lips were on mine, and she got her wish. I wouldn't have been able to form a single syllable word at that moment as fire rushed through me, heating me in all the best places as she lifted my by the waist. We were still connected at the lips. I felt myself smiling into her kiss at that, a tiny analytical portion of my mind informing me about how sexy that was.

Then she unceremoniously planted me on the big four post bed that dominated the space, and crawled onto the bed on top of me like a feline on the prowl and dominated 'my' space. Oh yes, please a thousand times.

She wiped a tear from my cheek tenderly as she lowered her lips down to mine again and shared a promise with me, though the contact that broke something inside of me, the chains that had been inside me my entire life. I pushed my lips desperately against hers as her tongue danced around mine. She had freed my passion, and just like a genie, it was impossible to put it back in the bottle.

I swallowed and grinned at her, I had never felt so aroused, so... complete, in my entire existence. Then she showed me what someone who had spent their life working with their hands could do with those magical hands. I moaned in pleasure, and not for the last time that night.

Chapter 10 – Feeling Sheepish

I remember that morning fondly. Waking up with a satisfied smile on my face, aching in the most wonderful ways, then my eyes flying wide when I learned that Hunter wasn't done with me yet. Oh the things she did to me. Purr.

After she let me out of bed, and I walked jelly-legged to the loo to clean up. Spontaneous giggle fits attacking me at each memory as I absently touched my lips, feeling the ghost of her kisses. I smelled my shoulder, her scent was all over my skin. She really had claimed me, hadn't she? I giggled again as I stretched.

The three of them accompanied me back to the Kennison's to help pack my bag and let the elder couple know I was heading back to London. I gave them most of my cash to tide them over until they could let the room over the garage again since I was leaving them in a lurch.

It struck me that I had dipped into my... special fund to do that. I didn't need it anymore. I finally didn't feel the urge to do that in case I needed to run. I looked at the tall redhead who was holding my suitcase like it was light as a purse. Hunter was my home. Then I looked at my brother and sister, my family. For the first time in my life, the anxiety and fear that pressed down upon me wasn't there, and I didn't know what to do with myself.

An hour later we were hoisting anchor and sailing down the Taff into Cardiff Bay into the gently blowing snow. The storm had lessened greatly by morning, leaving Cardiff blanketed in a sheet of white, which like London, wouldn't last long, but it gave a storybook cast to the city.

Once we left the locks of Cardiff Bay and sailed into the Bristol Channel, I learned how different it was to sail on the open seas than on the River Thames. There was a lot more deck movement and in some cases, choppy rolling of the boat as it slowly chugged its way from wave crest to wave crest. And... I absolutely loved it!

I felt so landlocked after I left London. I simply adored living on the water, and when firm ground was under my feet the past few months, it had felt as if something had been taken from me. So I stood out on the bow and just reveled in the water around me as the Deirdre made her way slowly south, down the coast until we could swing around to the east at Penzance.

Hunter often joined me there to wrap her arms possessively around me from behind, allowing me to sink back into her warmth as we just gazed across the coastline, reveling in our closeness.

Robert wouldn't let any of us take a turn at the wheel, he had taken to it like a duck to water. Hunter told me that he was a natural. And absently spoke about letting him do the crossing of the Saint George Channel when we went to visit her Nana.

That single statement out of everything had me silently crying. Without realizing it, the woman had become family. She saw us like family and didn't even think about us not being there when she kept her word to her Nana. I wasn't falling for the frustrating woman. It was all past tense. I had fallen so completely for her that it would have scared me, but hey... like Christine said, just look at that arse.

What was just a three-hour automobile ride from Cardiff to London, took us the better part of two days as we circled the coastline half way around Great Britain. It was a trip I would take a thousand times with Hunter. She made me wish the trip was exponentially longer. Hunter seemed to always be working blow decks when she wasn't showing me things about myself I hadn't imagine possible, and she didn't allow any of us to see what she was working on down in the hold.

We would occasionally spell Robert in the wheelhouse when Christine had meals ready. And he grumbled when McGrath sent him below to catch up on his homework. I learned that he was attending his tenth year at a secondary school just north of the Hammersmith, in the London core, and apparently he believed that McGrath was part of the great homework conspiracy.

Her response was succinct, "You wanted to come collect yer contrary sister instead of stayin' with Miss Doshi, that doesn't get ya out of the classes you're missin' now does it?"

Now that was something. Apparently, Robert's conflicted feelings were all bluster if he insisted on making the trek to Cardiff, on perhaps the slowest ship on the waves. It gave me hope I could make amends for my absence sooner rather than later.

Christine had informed me that our little brother had a monumental crush on Paya and I had to chuckle at that. I mean, who didn't? It must be in the Elgin genes or something. I missed her and Angie so much.

And that line of thinking brought on the anxiety as we slowly chugged up the River Thames, McGrath at the wheel as we slid up to Flotilla Pier in the last slip beside the Jabberwocky, where Angie, Stephanie, the roos, Tabitha, Teresa, and even June and Vanessa were all looking on.

I had an urge to tell Hunter to keep sailing up the river to Hammersmith so I could avoid the uncomfortable disapproval I was likely to receive from the women I respected the most. I sucked up my courage and stood beside my Amazonian Irishwoman. She sensed my apprehension and pulled me to her, wrapping an arm around my shoulders and kissing the top of my head.

My traitorous siblings and my... girlfriend, all stood back and waited as I crossed over the gap between the Deirdre and the dock, lending me no support. I felt like a sailor on a pirate ship, walking the plank to my doom in shark infested waters.

I swallowed as I stepped onto the sturdily constructed Flotilla Pier directly in front of Angie. I couldn't meet her eyes as we stood there facing each other silently. I couldn't handle it so I squeaked out, feeling sheepish and terrified as I said, “Ummm... hi?”

I thought my greatest fears had been realized when she didn't say anything for the longest heartbeat. I thought I had disappointed her beyond my capability to repair the relationship. Then I glurked as she reached out and yanked me to her, almost sobbing out, "Lenore."

I sobbed into her shoulder as she hugged me and mumbled out into her blouse, "I'm so sorry."

She was shaking her head as she hugged me then she kissed the top of my head and held me at arm's length to look me up and down. "Are you alright?'

I just nodded as I looked at her through watery eyes. I chuckled as I wiped my tears onto my coat sleeve as two roos attached themselves to my waist, their little grins and eager eyes turned up to me. I crouched. "Hey, mischief makers." I gave them proper hugs before I stood.

Steph leaned in, her involuntary facial ticks causing her left eye to twitch as she gave me a hug and a kiss on the cheek, then said, "The kids missed you, especially the big kid." Ange shoved her shoulder playfully.

I turned to find Paya standing there, her arms crossed defiantly across her chest, her expression stern. She screwed up her face and blew an errant strand of hair, which had escaped her well-maintained ponytail, out of her face then grumped out, "Don't you ever do that to us again."

I heard Tabby teasing in a whisper to the others, "Grumpy Paya is grumpy." Which just got her a slap to the back of her head by her wife who couldn't help but smile at her girl's shenanigans.

I looked at the Indian-Brit who had an expectant look on her face, I lowered my eyes and played with my hands nervously as I said in a whisper, “Yes Paya.”

Her stern face broke into a wide grin as she said, “There's a girl.” Then Paya wrapped her arms around me, pinning my arms to my side as she rocked me back and forth saying, “Ange was a mess without you, she missed you. I didn't miss you one bit.”

She kept rocking me back and forth, belying her words as Tabby snorted, “Yeah if worrying herself into a hole isn't missing you.”

Paya still didn't release me as she looked over to the rocker chick, “You are not helping here Tabs, you blustering lout.”

Tabby, not one to miss a beat or a quip, provided instantly, “That's why you love me.”

Paya parried. “Much to my chagrin, you have a valid point. Now shush, I'm hugging our Speedy.”

Tab's grinned, her copper eyes twinkling as she pantomimed locking her lips and throwing away the key as Teresa rolled her eyes at her. I had so missed their banter.

Then when Paya was satisfied with her silent hug chastising of her misbehaving runner she released me then grumped up her face again to hide her smile. McGrath's term 'criminally cute' came to mind.

I shrugged, not knowing what to say and so just apologized again, “I'm sorry. I promise I'll do better.”

She nodded once and with that out of the way everyone was in motion, passing out hugs to me and my siblings and girl as they crossed over to the dock. I couldn't stop the tears from flowing. Those happy tears.

We retired to the Persephone for a bit to discuss my misadventure and what had gone on at the Flotilla in my absence while Paya tried to feed us all. McGrath used that as our cue. "As much as we'd like to stay and eat with you wonderful women and wee ones, It's comin' on high tide, and we need ta get the Deirdre tucked in fer the night. And Bobby has school in the mornin' while the rest of us have a lot ta do to prepare for the grand openin' on Friday."

She pointed at Paya to stop her as she opened her mouth. "You have mahy solemn oath that I'll feed the surly lot when we drop anchor."

Paya grinned cutely at that, and I saw Robert blush profusely at that grin. He had it bad. Didn't he know she was twice his age? She turned the grin on me, and I blushed and looked down. Shite, me too.

McGrath glanced at me and said, "We'll be needin' to do a supply run in the mornin', Frizzy. So it'd be best if ya take the truck and meet us there."

Ange stepped forward to defend me when she called me Frizzy but froze when the infuriating Irishwoman leaned down and gave me a tender kiss that had my toes curling and my smile blooming as I heated up in all the most interesting places.

I looked over, and Angie was stunned. She was just standing there blinking at us with her mouth hanging open. Steph looked at her and us then with a silly grin she reached up and nudged her girl's mouth shut.

Paya looked like she was going to burst into rainbows and glitter as she bounced on her toes and said, "So it's like that is it? It's about time!"

Then she looked back to my cabin then at McGrath then me and asked. "Umm... so you're staying on the Deirdre then?"

Ok, if it is possible to blush yourself into a puddle, I had to be right on the cusp of that event as my cheeks burned and I turned to bury my face into Hunter's shoulder as I nodded. The evil ones in the cabin gave a silly cheer, and I muttered, "Wood chipper for all of you." They laughed.

I took a deep breath, taking in the scent of sawdust, grease, and soap and exhaled as I straightened and looked at Paya. "Yes. I might be moving out of the pilot house... if McGrath will have me."

I looked up to those hazel eyes, and they were twinkling in mirth as she remained silent. I backhanded her iron gut, and she broke into her smarmy smirk and said softly, letting her Tweedledee out to play, "Of course I'll be havin' ya on the Deirdre, darlin'." I wanted to die of embarrassment at the double entendre, but it thrilled me all the same as I found myself nodding at her, feeling like a schoolgirl with her crush.

Tabs snagged the truck keys of their peg and tossed them

toward my back, I reached back and caught them and shot her a challenge with a cocked eyebrow. I was no match for her restrained, over-amused smile.

I looked up at Hunter and bounced to my tiptoes and gave her a quick peck on the lips and said, “See you at the Hammersmith?”

She responded jovially, “Not if I see you first.” Then she added before I could threaten her, “Darlin'.” I melted.

Christine stepped beside me, Robert at her back and she informed McGrath instead of me. “We'll ride with Len.”

I cringed at the chorus of the peanut gallery as they instantly blurted, “No!”

Hunter just shrugged with a grin and said, “It's your funeral. Now use your manners.”

I had to chuckle as my siblings turned and said goodnight to everyone. She was acting like a surrogate mum. She nudged my back. “Why are ya grinnin' like that? You too.”

I shot her a death glare which seemed to make her oddly pleased then I went around handing out hugs, thanks, and goodbyes.

I heard a collective snort when Bobby pulled me out the door with urgency saying, “If we hurry, maybe we can beat McGrath to the Hammersmith.” I thought, 'challenge accepted' as I raised my hand behind me and just barely aborted flipping them all off when I remembered the roos were there. So I settled on waving them off. If I were such a bad driver, then why have I never been in an accident? I put that to you.

We beat Hunter... by a long shot. My brother and sister were oddly silent as they just sat and breathed purposefully in the cab of the truck as we saw the Deirdre slide into her mooring area, and McGrath dropped anchor.

Then my siblings bolted out of the truck without a how do you do, and ran over to the retaining wall along the Lower Mall promenade, as Hunter lowered the gangplank and stepped across. I shook my head and followed wondering what had gotten into them.

Christine was taking up some of my mannerisms as she lightly backhanded the Irish handywoman in the gut as she arrived by her and accused, "How could you let us take our lives into our hands like that? I thought you were supposed to be our protector."

Hunter was nothing but toothy grins as Bobby just stalked past her and onto the boat as he silently shook his head at her in disapproval. I narrowed my eyes and accused in a petulant tone, "Not you two too. There's nothing wrong with my driving. And you wanted to beat the leprechaun here didn't you?" They didn't even look at me, the traitors. But whatever, I won.

I didn't even stop at my girl, twapping her gut as I stalked past. I smiled to myself at her burst of laughter as she followed then my feet left the deck as she wrapped her arms around my waist from behind and lifted me to bury her face into the crook of my neck from behind.

Good lord... a thrill of lust and excitement burned its way

through me from the point of contact of her hot lips on my neck. I involuntarily cocked my head to give her better access as I melted in her arms. I squeaked out, “Ok, I forgive you.”

She set me down and strode past with a smug look on her face as she said, “Thought you might, Frizzy.” I narrowed my eyes and hustled after her as I tried to fight off my smile. She was so going to pay for that.

Tina gave in to letting me help her prepare supper, and before long we were all laughing and talking at the table as we ate. I asked more questions about Bobby's school since he had to get up early with the rest of us to beat low tide to get to class. I asked if there was anyone special he had his eye on there.

He blushed. There was! Christina said in a dreamy voice, “Allie Porter.” She made a heart beating motion with the hands pressed to her chest. My brother grinned down then threw a carrot chunk at her, and we all chuckled. Young love was so cute.

As we finished cleaning up after the meal and moved to the seating area, which I just now realized didn't have a telly, the boat began to creak and lean a bit. My siblings and Hunter seemed to just flex with it as I grabbed the couch to maintain my balance as I sat down heavily and grabbed onto the armrest. There was an odd swishing and grinding sound and then nothing.

McGrath gave me a playful grin and explained as she placed her arm over my shoulders and pulled me into her, “Low tide. Yer stuck with me for the duration now.” I acquiesced that it wasn't an unpleasant situation to find oneself in as I snuggled into her.

Meanwhile, Tina plopped down on the other end of the couch, and Bobby sat in the oversized chair he preferred. I marveled at the fact that they were so relaxed and seemed perfectly at home here. And... happy.

I realized that I had Hunter to thank for it.

She had gone out of her way to help my family and give them a place to call home while I had hidden myself away in a city that wasn't everything I had made it out to be in my childish fantasies of escape.

We had a spirited discussion about a great many things, including to my surprise, a lot of Hunter's youth. She trusted my family with her secrets, and that endeared the still somehow mysterious woman to me even more. I wanted to spend every minute of every day unlocking those mysteries.

Then my girl stood on the oddly tilted deck and said, "Twenty minutes to lights out." My brother and sis groaned in protest but stood and gave us hugs good night and trudged down the tilted corridor to their rooms.

I was impressed with Bobby's room when I first saw it. Though spartan, it was larger than where Christine stayed in Hunter's old quarters. I knew it was important for teens to have a room of their own, their Fortresses of Solitude. Hell, I even had one in my childhood home, where I could step out onto the roof and wish to be anywhere but there.

When we retired to the master cabin, I stood there looking at this incredible woman who was seemingly chiseled from stone, and whispered the most frightening admission of my life, "I think I may be falling for you."

She lost all of her smarmy cockiness. Her smirk changed to something unreadable as she said while looking down at the nightshirt she had started pulling on. "Good ta know yer catchin' up with me then." She pulled the shirt on then just slid into bed like she hadn't just said that.

My eyes watered for some unfathomable reason as I smiled at her. Then I quickly got into one of her work tees that hung to my knees. It smelled delightfully like her.

I slid into the bed, and she automatically wrapped an arm around my waist and pulled me into an almost desperate cuddle. I sighed into her warmth, and we just lay there in silence. Sharing all that we were with each other, and it seemed the most intimate act I had ever experienced in my life.

I hugged the arm that was wrapped around me and let sleep sneak in and take me to dreams of worlds of carved wood and a certain exasperating woman with a pixie cut.

Chapter 11 – Masterpiece

The next couple days were the most hectic days of my life, and most frustrating since Hunter locked herself away in the hold of the ship to work on her secret project whenever we weren't at the Steinberg, or I wasn't running for the Flotilla. The girls had made a mess of my system, and it would take weeks for me to get everything running smoothly again.

I had forgotten just how much I loved the people that we helped with the Flotilla and Slingshot programs, and they welcomed me back with open arms. I worked twice as diligently on the final steps of the renovation to earn their respect back. I couldn't believe how much was accomplished when I was gone. The place looked amazing. It felt as if I had stepped back in time a hundred years when walking the halls of the Steinberg.

The final project was up on the roof. In outright defiance of Mr. Hasting's edict, Paya and McGrath had conspired to swap out the pergola and seating area on the roof with a spectacular replacement. The pavers were replaced with old cobblestones that were taken from a nearby street renovation project and repurposed for the patio under the expanded pergola.

The structure itself looked to be an antique, a much bigger wood construction which looked like it had been taken from a forgotten rose garden of a posh estate somewhere. The center of each arch was adorned by a hand-carved rose and carved thorny vines spiraled down the four corner-posts which held the upper latticework up.

I wondered for a moment if Hunter had carved them, if it were the secret project she wouldn't allow us Elgins to see. But I dissuaded myself of that as the crescent-shaped board I had seen the first time I was on the Deirdre, was much larger, and these were weathered and cracked from age, and meticulously restored to their former glory.

It had to have been one of McGrath's historical rescues. One of the pieces she spoke to and assured she would find a new home for. I understood her better now, and I found her eccentricity of speaking with the forgotten works of others to be reassuring to me in some way.

I looked around the rooftop, knowing that there would be someone a century from now who would honor the memory of the blood sweat, tears, and love that our little group had put into the Steinberg. Someone just like Hunter who spoke to the past through the craftsmanship.

The group opted to take our final lunch before the building officially opened to the residents in the morning, up in the freezing winter day, on that outdoor roof oasis which would serve the tenants of the building well for years. Paya had shared the plans for a little rooftop community garden that would be installed come spring. Because as our ever smiling Indian-Brit leader had said, “Every home needs a green space.”

We had anticipated our people's desire to eat there, and I stepped around to fire up the standing propane heaters we had placed strategically around the perimeter of the patio to keep it warm as some helpers started streaming up the roof stairs. I smiled as I recognized almost all of them as people we placed in the Slingshot Program previously.

That's when Mr. Hastings showed up to throw a bucket of cold water on us. The man appeared at the door to the stairs and looked out across the roof, his brows knotted and eyes narrowed in disapproval.

Paya muttered, "Oh, just great." Then she plastered on one of her patented innocent faces as she moved to intercept the red-faced man as he stalked toward us. The impromptu worker's celebration silenced.

Those of us the group affectionately called "upper management" flanked our fearless leader. Angie and Christine on her right and McGrath and I on her left. Bobby would have been there in support too if he hadn't been in school.

I had to smile as I saw Mrs. Smythe looming in the door behind Hastings, holding a tray of sandwiches as her eyes narrowed at his back. She was as always, in a smartly pressed professional suit.

When the man met Paya half way to the patio, he started blustering, "Miss Doshi, I must take exception to this blatant violation of the Office of Historic Preservation guidelines in regards to this monstrosity.

Before Paya could speak, my sister blurted out, "It's just a space for the future tenants to come out to enjoy the fresh..."

The man actually snapped at her, he must have reached some sort of breaking point, “Hold your tongue, stupid girl. This blatant disre...”

I caught the familiar flinch of my sister when he snapped at her and her squinted eye waiting for the hand to lash out to strike her and a fire exploded inside me. Rationally I knew this man was not my father, and he wasn't about to strike her, but verbal abuse was just as damaging as any fist. I was so afraid and broken before, but I wasn't that child who couldn't defend herself or her sibling anymore.

No more!

I stepped forward and glared at the man, my hands balled into fists and interrupted him mid-sentence, “There was no call for that verbal abuse, Mr. Hastings. I don't give a flying fuck that your delicate sensibilities were hurt by the people here wanting an outdoor space, because nobody, and I mean nobody gets to disabuse my sister. Do I make myself clear... sir?”

I was almost shaking with rage and the cathartic release of something inside of me. That scared little girl who cringed when she heard a raised voice or a loud sound. She was free now, and she was never going to hide in her corner again.

I glared at the man, and he visibly calmed, taking a breath then exhaling and nodding as he gained control of himself. In a much calmer tone, he said, “Of course.” He looked at Christine who was staring at me with bulging eyes and repeated, “Of course. My apologies, Miss. I'm just a bit out of sorts from Miss

Doshi and McGrath's tendencies to ignore my authority. It isn't an excuse, it was uncalled for and I shouldn't have snapped."

I inclined my head in acceptance of his apology as my sister crossed her arms over her chest and nodded as Angie looped her arms over her shoulder to pull Tina beside her. I relaxed backward as two strong hands rested on my shoulders, giving them a little squeeze. I leaned into the intoxicating scent of sawdust, grease, and soap.

Paya opened her mouth, but my girl beat her to it. "Come now Brent. Are ya sure that this is outside the guidelines? Think really hard on this. I can be schooling ya on it if ya like."

He looked between Paya, Hunter, and the pergola. He exhaled loudly in exasperation again and said, "Contrary to what you may believe Miss McGrath, my purpose in life is not to put up roadblocks for those wishing to restore historic buildings. It is by preserving history that we can learn and appreciate what came before us. So it can serve as an example and reminder to our children of the craftsmanship and artisan abilities of a bygone era, so it isn't forgotten to the annals of time."

His point made, he nudged his hand, face up toward the infraction on his ordered life and said, "By all means, instruct me on my folly."

McGrath stepped around me to his side and turned to look at the gorgeous new patio setup, all of our people were looking on at her. She said, "Correct me if I'm wrong here, Brent, now doesn'a the guidelines of yer very office dictate that no modifications to a historic structure can be made which are not done for reasons of accessibility, without the review and express permission of the OHP. After an investigation inta how it may affect the original structure or integrity or historical consequence?"

I blinked, it was as if she were reciting something out of a book. The man nodded. She slapped him on the back. "Well, there ya have it then."

His brows furrowed, as did mine and probably most of our group's. He said, "I'm afraid you lost me when your trolley lost the rail back there."

She snorted and gave him her cocky smirk as she placed an arm across his shoulder and dragged him toward the pergola, us 'upper management' traveling in their wake. "Well I ask in all earnestness, how is this patio in any way modifyin' the structure? The pavers are simply layin' on the roof, and the pergola is sittin' on top. Nothin' was done to the structure. It's no different than havin' patio furniture sittin' on it, now is it?"

He opened his mouth then started to think as I blinked at her explanation. Then he shut his mouth as he tilted his head, brows furrowed. She was right, how was it any different than anything else you set inside a room? It didn't change the structure in any way, it was just functional decoration.

He started to nod and looked a little sheepish as he said as she released his shoulders as they stopped at the patio, "I hadn't thought of it in those terms. You are correct, this doesn't go against the dictates laid out in the OHP charter."

He had a sour look on his face, and McGrath smiled and said, "If it is any consolation Brent, I have these for ya..." She pulled out some papers from her coat pocket and handed them to the man. I leaned over to look as he looked through the papers.

They were photocopies of old newspaper clippings dated at the end of the eighteen hundreds. They were articles about tea parties thrown by society elites, or celebrations and fundraisers for politicians. They had pictures accompanying them. Each one was on a rooftop with a similar style patio set up for the event.

He spoke absently as he sifted through them, "We have historians digging diligently into the past of all the buildings under our preview, yet you always seem to find things we have missed, Miss McGrath. Where do you find this stuff? May I keep these?"

She nodded. "They're all yours. I think your group is sometimes a little too focused and are lookin' specifically for articles about the buildin's. What ya seem to forget is that the buildin's are part of the city, part of London. They are always there, the backdrop to life, to history. So all you have to do is look for that life, for the events, and there in the background will be the buildin's that make up the foundations of our lives."

She shrugged. "You look for the buildin's, I look for the life that happened around them, and know they will always be there. I just searched for rooftop events in the archives, and that's what I found."

So that's what she does at the Royal Library Archive!

He nodded and she prompted, “So we're square now?”

He looked around again and said in defeat, “Yes. We're good.”

There was an awkward silence for a couple seconds before Paya chirped out, “Yeah, what she said.” A chuckle rolled through the little crowd, and I couldn't help but smile at the woman bouncing on her toes with a pleased grin on her face.

Then she offered an olive branch to the man. “Please, Mr. Hastings, won't you join us for lunch? It is our final hurrah before the grand opening tomorrow.”

He nodded saying, “It would be my pleasure, Miss Doshi.”

Hunter reached over to grab a fizzy pop from a folding table and popped the top as she said, “You'll need your strength for what you see in the mornin', you'll likely burst a blood vessel.” Then she chugged the drink and turned to me as the man stood there in abject horror.

I couldn't help wondering just what she had planned that was going to cause the man more consternation than this. I chuckled as he asked Paya, “What does she mean by that?” He turned around and asked nobody in particular, “What did she mean by that?” Then he slumped and grabbed a drink himself as he muttered, “Oh bloody hell.”

I grinned up at the smarmy looking Irishwoman and reached up to run my fingers through her silky hair and feel the little hairs from the shaved portion gently scratching at my palm. “It's sort of hot when you aren't aiming your mean streak at me.”

She shrugged and smirked, "Says you, Frizzy."

Argh! I was trying to compliment her then she has to tease. I muttered, "Yeah, says me, Hunter."

I cringed when Angie leaned in toward us, eyes wide, "Did you just call her Hunter?" Then she added in thought, "The contracts... H. McGrath." The smile was splitting her face.

I face-palmed, and my girl growled down at me and my big mouth. Then I tried to slink away when Paya joined us, "Who's Hunter?"

I squeaked when I was tugged back to my girl and onto my tiptoes as she pulled me to her side and muttered as she shook her head in resignation and looked down at me with a cocked eyebrow of doom, "Just... lovely."

I squinted one eye and squished up my face in apology, "Sorry?"

She winked. "Yer gonna be." Oh. A promise. Yes, please. I grinned.

She sighed heavily and dragged me away to the food while Angie bounced on her toes with a wicked gleam in her eye as she told Paya, "McGrath is."

I tried so very hard not to snort when Paya's response was nothing but a silly, "Oooo."

Fine. I snorted.

***

The next morning, Saturday, I woke up grumpy without my favorite bedwarmer pulling me tightly to her. She had dropped us siblings Elgin off at the Persephone, to use my old unused cabin. She said she had a special project she had to set up before the opening ceremony. The evil woman had shut off her mobile so she could work undisturbed and I missed the aggravating sound of her voice.

Paya and Angie left us around midnight after Paya had a heated conversation with the city council about the opening ceremony. They wanted another wave of inspections in an attempt to appease the Hammersmith Borough Council who were still convinced we would be bringing unsavories into their neighborhood. Anything to put off the certificate of occupancy until they could come up with another roadblock.

It is amazing to me how quickly our fearless leader can switch off the warmest personality that God has seen fit to install into one of his creations and go into cutthroat business mode. She was ruthless, and I can see why June respects Paya's ability to make waves as well as she does here in London. Both women are primal forces of nature. The city caved.

I rolled over and shook Christine's shoulder. “Come on Peanut, time to get ready, we have a building to open.” She groaned in protest.

I sat up and looked at the Robert shaped lump under a stack of blankets and pillows on the floor and threw a pillow at it. Direct hit! I got a matching groan from him. I liked playing the evil big sis. I clapped my hands together. “Right then, come on you two lazybones, we have to be at the Steinberg in just over an hour.”

Bobby stood, blankets sloughing off of him and onto the floor as he groaned again, scratching his head as he trudged toward the loo like a zombie. I grinned. "There's a boy." I snorted as he shot me the international sign of greeting. "Is that any way to respect your elders?" I made a borking sound as a pillow smacked my face from the side. I was being teamed up on!

I rolled to my feet out of bed and bent to tidy the nest Bob left. My ruse successful, I tossed my discarded pillow at Christine and scored a direct hit, and she humorously just flopped back onto the bed. I said, "Be a doll and tidy the bed."

I started to think I was a bad influence on my siblings as she displayed the same hand sign my brother just had. I really had to stop flipping people off and swearing around my family. I was such a bad role model. Not that they got much else from me as they both had a habit of emulating McGrath. Oh Lord preserve us all if there were three McGraths in the world.

I had to force a smile off my face when I thought of the aggravating and sexy handywoman. She'd be the death of me yet, I was sure of it, but what a way to go.

Just as we were finishing up getting ready for the day and moving out to the pilot house to get our caffeine wake up from the freshly brewed pot of coffee, our ride showed up. Paya strode in and almost sang, "Good morning my lovelies."

The kids gave silly waves, and I stole a page out of Tabby's book and replied, "Hiya Paya." She gave a hop and landed in front of me smiling at the coffee mug in my hand. I rolled my eyes at her and handed her the mug and filled another one for myself.

She said as she sipped, “I knew there was a reason I loved you.” I blushed and then she cocked her head, “You know, Hunter is good for you. You smile more now when you aren't plotting her demise. And I love that you let your hair down now.”

I absently touched my hair, I rarely ever put it in a ponytail anymore. I blushed, knowing my girl liked it down, and that's all it took to get over my insecurity about it. I wore it down all the time for her.

I just shrugged noncommittally which got me the expected eye roll from her. I took a couple deep pulls at the coffee, letting the hot liquid start warming me from the inside, giving it a chance to wake me. The scintillating aroma was waking my other senses. Then she said, holding up her keys, “Come on brats, time to start the next evolution of the Flotilla.”

I set my cup down and grabbed for the keys, “Right, I'll drive.”

She yanked the keys out of my reach, her eyes bulging wide as they all shouted in unison, “No!”

I blew the hair out of my face and grabbed my coat as I trudged past all the traitors. “I hate you all, my driving isn't that bad.”

As they all hustled after me, I had to grin as Robert stated, “Yes it is.”

I was in a hurry. I needed a surly leprechaun fix. It was so odd how I had gotten so used to having her around, to having someone in my life who I... loved so very much. Yes, fine I said it, I love Hunter McGrath, are you happy now?

We arrived in the shadow o the Hammersmith a few minutes later. In like twice the time it took me to get there since Paya drove like an old lady. I noted the Deirdre was resting on the bank at low tide. The service truck my girl stole from me for the prior night was nowhere to be seen down on Lower Mall.

I didn't know why she needed it since she was in easy walking distance of the Steinberg. Whatever her secret project was, it had better be worth it.

I wanted to reach my foot over and slam it down on the gas pedal to make Paya go a respectable speed.

Though I admit it was fun listening to my brother and sister sing with her along the way. At least some Elgin's could carry a note unlike me. I enjoyed seeing my siblings happy. Their smiles had been so rare back then, before...

I swear the tiny smirk on Paya's lips was because she knew our sedate speed was driving me crazy. I mean, like just now when she waited for those vehicles to pass before turning onto the lane in front of the Steinberg. I totally could have made it between the gap between cars.

We had to park a block away because the street was lined with vehicles and there was a large group of people gathered outside the entry doors which had a big red ribbon across them. We bundled up and stepped out into the cold and slushy ground, then made our way to the front.

Our evil compatriots were there. I scanned the crowd of people standing on the slushy walk, looking for a familiar pixie cut. I realized that I recognized most of the people in attendance. They were past and future people and families we had placed through the Slingshot program, the residents of the Flotilla, and even our extended group of misfits through June's people from London Harmony.

And standing beside Angie, Stephanie, and the roos, was Mrs. Jones, Mr. Hastings, and a man I didn't know, but looked vaguely familiar.

I stepped up to Ange and whispered as I scanned the crowd, worry in my voice. “Where's McGrath?”

She shrugged and nudged her chin, I followed her gaze as she said, “The supply truck is up front there. She isn't answering her mobile.”

I nodded. “She turned it off. Said she had a lot of work to do and couldn't be distracted.”

I hadn't realized how anxious I had been until the door opened a little bit, and an exhausted looking Hunter slipped out. She gave an embarrassed look, and ducked under the ribbon and slid to my side. She whispered to the group, “Sorry, took a little longer than I expected.”

Paya narrowed an eye in suspicion as she hugged my girl. “What did you do...” She paused and then added, “Hunter?”

My Irishwoman exhaled and squinted an eye at me as she said

accusingly, "And this is why we can't have nice things." She cut my snarky barb short by kissing me. I melted into her like I did every time. How can such a simple action give me such pleasure? Her lips felt like home to me.

She glanced over to a beaming Paya who looked like she was going to explode into rainbows and little hearts as she watched us. Then she said to my silly boss, "Just mahy gift ta the Flotilla. I gave the buldin' back her heart."

Cryptic much? I dusted sawdust and wood shavings off of the heavy flannel shirt she was wearing last night and looked down at her tool belt. She had been up all night?

She avoided any other questions by turning her attention back to me. "How was yer night, darlin'?"

I shrugged and said in a small voice, "Missed you."

She wiggled her eyebrows. "What's not ta miss?"

I exhaled in exasperation. "I don't know why I love you so much."

She froze, I froze, and it felt like everyone around us turned to look, I'm sure it was just my imagination. She had a sort of goofy look on her face, and I swear a million eyes were on us, and I turned from her as she started to say something and I chastised, "What are you all gawking at? I love my girlfriend, is that a crime?"

Everyone was all grins and smiles. I turned back to Hunter as I felt myself blushing profusely, my face afire. She started, "You..."

I held up a finger. “Shut up.”

She closed her mouth for a moment, then she opened it again, and I pointed a warning finger at her. “Not a single solitary word.”

She paused but went to speak anyway, I shoved my finger at her, and she closed her mouth then gave me her signature cocky smirk. I said, “Don't get too full of yourself, you tosser.”

Angie cleared her throat, and I winced and pulled a quid from my pocket and handed it to her as I shot the roos a sheepish apology. They giggled.

Then I looked back at Hunter, and she sighed and said, “I love you too, Lenore.” A little cheer went up and she hugged me, and the roos thought hat was great fun so they attacked our hips with hugs of their own. I smiled down at them and patted Natalie's knitted winter hat.

Paya said to the crowd, “It looks as though we have two things to celebrate today.” A chuckle rippled around us as I blushed into my girl's shoulder.

Paya looked so posh and polished in her own designer business suit. She was always so put together, nothing out of place and not even a seam misaligned. She reached over for the huge set of scissors leaning against the doorframe as she cleared her throat loudly. The murmuring of the crowd settled in anticipation as she said, “Before the mayor of our fine city, Leonard Abney, performs the ribbon cutting ceremony for the first of what I hope is many multifamily dwellings for the Flotilla

Project, I'd like to say a few words."

Oh hey, that other bloke was the Mayor? I guess I should have known that. I felt a little sheepish just then. Paya handed the scissors to the man as he stepped to her side. The middle-aged man with the silvering mane of hair towered over her in his smart three-piece suit. His cufflinks gleamed in the sparse light filtering through the cloudy sky.

Paya looked about, over the eager faces and said, "This is the culmination of hard work from many people giving of themselves so others can have pride in themselves as they get back on their feet. I am so very proud of each and every individual who supported this effort, to help out the people I see as my friends and family, in their time of need."

She was tearing up, and God help me if my eyes weren't getting a little watery too. She loved these people so much, and it was quite apparent that there was no better person to head up the Flotilla. She cared so much for those less fortunate than herself, and she respected each and every one of them... of us.

She was one of the rare ones who saw the invisible people on the streets, and her heart went out to them. I had more respect for her and Angie than anyone else I had ever met. Their passion for people rivaled Hunter's passion for history and the spirit of the wood she worked with.

I tuned back in as she was finishing up, there were a lot of tears around me, and I wondered what I had missed when I was reflecting about her. She ended it with, "And I'd like to extend special thanks to the woman who worked all of our fingers to the bone and kept us on task for the entire renovation. Her skill and insight were invaluable to help restore the Steinberg to her former glory..."

She motioned up to the exterior of the building which couldn't have looked better than the day it first opened all those years ago, in a different era. It looked timeless, right down to the meticulously restored wings adorning the upper parapet.

She finished with, "Your slave driver and mine, McGrath." A cheer went up, and my girl graciously gave her an acknowledging head tilt. I could feel all her muscles tighten, she was uncomfortable with the spotlight on her. It was odd to me that I knew someone so well that I knew that she would prefer the building get the attention, not her. She feels she was just a tool which just helped coax the history and majesty out of it.

Then Paya looked over to the Mayor as she carefully wiped her eyes to avoid smearing her mascara, "Mister Abney?"

He smiled down at her softly, she had even moved the big man. He turned and gave a crooked smile to the people gathered about. "Well then. I don't know how to top that." We all chuckled as Hunter snagged our fearless leader and pulled her into a silly three-way hug. She knew Paya needed the contact as well as I did. Ange had her hand on Paya's arm as if to say, "we are here" to her.

Abney just shrugged and winked to the group. "So with no further ado, I'm happy to say that the Steinberg is open for business." Then he cut the ribbon and everyone cheered.

I can't explain how happy I was at that moment. It was just a building, right? Why was I so thrilled? Was it that people I knew were going to be able to stand back up on their own two feet in the flats inside, or was it this odd pride I had inside me, knowing that I had helped to make it possible. Something I accomplished with my own hands.

We stood back as a couple reporters mixed in the crowd took pictures of the mayor at the door and shots of him shaking Paya's hand.

Angie moved to the doors and brought two fingers to her lips and whistled shrilly. Everyone turned, and she said loudly, "Shall we move this party inside now?" She got more cheering as our group of 'upper management' joined her.

Most of us were intimately familiar with the inside of the building, having put in hours of work restoring it. But I was humming with the anticipation of seeing the reactions from the ones who hadn't seen the majesty of what was to most, just a simple apartment block, which most might have thought should have been torn down and a modern structure put in its place long ago.

But a newer building wouldn't have the warmth, the... soul of the Steinberg. I understood the woman I loved more and more each day.

Angie and Paya flung the doors wide with a flourish, and we all started to stream in, then stumbled to a halt with a collective gasp. My jaw dropped, and I gasped at an incredible sight I which had not been there in the main lobby just a day before.

The arched ceiling in this area had always seemed so open compared to the rest of the corridor, and Hunter had gone through great pains to maintain the oddly angled blocks on the floor, high on the walls and at the apex of the ceiling. Was this truly what they were for?

Hastings pushed in front of us all as we just stared at a masterpiece of woodworking. He stepped over to one of the anchor points with a look of combined horror and amazement on his face.

I turned to Hunter, all eyes were swinging between her and the new addition to the lobby. She shrugged and blushed, causing her freckles to stand out on her face as she said, "Tis the heart of the Steinberg, I couldn't get it back, so I made her a new one."

She pulled out a frayed piece of paper from her pocket, beckoning Mr. Hastings over with a nudge of her chin. She said to him as she unfolded the paper to display a newspaper article dated nineteen sixty-one. "Now before ya getting' yer knickers in a bunch, Brent, take a look here."

The article was about a fundraiser for a barrister's bid to become judge, it was thrown by a high society family who owned various buildings around the city. I recognized the lobby the picture was taken in. It was the Steinberg!

The focus was on the barrister and the socialite shaking hands in a crowd in the lobby, and in the background, all grainy and blurred was an arched construct like the one which dominated the lobby now. The one people were streaming around us and into the lobby to gawk at its expertly carved wood.

She explained, "I stumbled upon this the day after I accepted the job here. I had to know about this." She pointed at the picture then at the amazing construct.

It looked to be a giant carved birdcage that had a lot of the same features throughout the building, like the huge wings outside and the ones on the cage to the lift. They were great sweeping wings whose feathers connected to the anchors. The sweeping arcs all came together, soaring overhead to connect at a great wooden wreath, which itself was made of beautifully carved feathers.

She said, "I tracked down the previous owners before Gordon Leavens bought it. The man was the great-grandson of the man who commissioned the buildin'. He shared a beautiful tale with me. Henry Steinberg was a real estate mogul in the late eighteen hundreds. His wife had passed away at the young age of fifty-nine shortly before the buildin' was commissioned."

She hugged me to her as she released the news article to Hastings. "Janice Steinberg had loved her birds more than anything and so Henry wished to honor her memory, and he themed the Steinberg with the cages and the wings that represented the birds she loved and the angel wings he knew she would soar with in Heaven. He called the cage the heart of the Steinberg."

She pointed at the birdcage that dominated the space. “When the family went to renovate the buildin' in the sixties, to modernize it, a friend of theirs, Baron Slipton, had coveted the cage and gave them an offer they couldn't refuse. He took the heart of the Steinberg away and had it installed in his estates near the Slipton Castle up north. The family wouldn't grant me permission ta go look at it.”

Then she shrugged. “I couldn't give her heart back, but I did the best I could to reproduce it with that one grainy photograph.”

Paya was speaking in a faraway voice as she just stood there, staring up at the crown of the arches, “It's beautiful, McGrath.” I nodded my agreement.

She restored the building's heart to it, it may not be the same, but she had poured her own heart into it to make sure a plain building like this had it's grand centerpiece back, to give it its character, its own life.

She looked over at Hastings who was squinting at the picture then looking at the carved masterpiece. He paused and looked at her and nodded. Then he shook his head. “I still don't know how you find this stuff, but yes. I'll sign off on this.”

He reached out to run his hand along the carvings and then said almost like it tore his soul out to admit it, “Connor would be proud.”

She exhaled as her hands tensed. She said, “Thank you, Mr. Hastings.” His eyes widened slightly, it was the first time she had not called him Brent.

He inclined his head in acknowledgment then my Amazonian leprechaun was grinning at me as she dragged me down the corridor toward the catering stations at the end. “Let's eat, I've had nothin' all night. I'm starvin' and exhausted. Then I need ta get ya back to our bed.”

I blushed and squeaked out to this wondrous woman, “Ok.”

Then she had to go and ruin the mood by adding, “Frizzy.”

I grumped through a grin as I followed along, “Shamrock surfer.”

Epilogue

As Lenore and I brought the Deirdre into port, I yelled out the window ta Bobby, "Secure the lines!" She was surprisingly adept at pilotin' a ship compared to the way she took every other driver's lives inta her hands when she got behind the wheel of the Flotilla's truck.

The lanky boy called back as he hopped over to the dock with a mooring line, "On it, McGrath!"

We had ta wait till spring ta navigate the open seas ta mahy homeland. I felt bad. It was comin' on two years past my promised visit ta Nana. I had so many times thought just ta fly over but it just didn't feel right, leavin' the Deirdre behind.

I had to grin at the reason my heart beat as she shut down the engine and checked the board. Her wild, curly hair, was beckonin' and teasin'. Just darin' me ta run mahy hands through the silky locks and get them tangled in those delightful waves.

I gave in and reached one hand out and slid it through Lenore's hair to cup the back of her head as she leaned back onto my hand, closed her eyes, and moaned. That moan vibrated through mahy hand and down into my core where it re-stoked that fire that burned deep inside whenever she was around.

I smiled. The scrappy woman owned me, and I'd never felt happier to be owned in mahy life. Nobody had ever been able to dish out the shite I served up and throw it back at me, and that excited me in ways it probably shouldn't. She kept me honest.

I looked down and smiled at Christine who was throwin' the stern line to her brother. I can't imagine mahy life without the three of them onboard. Len's siblings felt like family to me. I reveled in it. I had always been an only child, and now I couldn't imagine not havin' mahy surrogate little brother and sister around.

I pulled Lenore to me with that hand cupping the back of her head, and I kissed her with the passion she kindled inside of me. Showing her that I returned that passion back, tenfold. The little runt could kiss. She melted into me the way only she could, surrenderin' herself to me, openin' herself up ta me in a way that implied implicit trust that I could hold her heart for her. That was so sexy and arousin' ta me.

She was my smile, so I smiled into our kiss, and she started smiling too as she pulled back slightly and asked, “What?”

I shrugged and said, “Nothin', I just love ya.”

She exhaled in a sigh and said in a tone that can't be faked, “I love you too.”

Then she smirked. “You're ok for an unruly Irishwoman.”

I chuckled. “If you say so, Fuzzy.” She backhanded my gut then paused to trace my abdomen muscles as she bit her lower lip.

I swallowed hard as I started to heat up. “Don't go startin' what ya can't finish. Me Nana is expectin' us.”

She gave me a cruel smirk as she stepped away, trailin' a finger along my stomach. “Your loss.” Yes. Yes, it most certainly was. The little wretch.

I gave her a smirk and then said, “You're awfully full of

yerself." Then I looked out the window and pointed up the hill to the little brick house on the rise. A woman stood on the porch, leanin' against a support post. "She's waitin'."

Lenore got suddenly nervous and absently smoothed back her curls. A nervous habit she had that was sort of endearin' ta me. It showed the cracks in her bravado.

She was wearing a dress, she looked good in dresses, but she rarely wore them. She was nervous about meetin' Nana so she wanted ta look her best. We secured the cabin then I offered an arm to her, and she took it and we headed out with the kids to visit the woman who brought me Ma into this world.

***

It was late that night when Nana asked me ta her room. She had hit it off spectacularly with Lenore, who was so nervous I was afraid she was goin' ta vomit. And Nana doted over the kids, makin' them eat their fill twofold at suppertime.

I followed her to her bureau, and she pulled out a little box and said, "Yer mother, God rest her soul, held me to a promise to make sure ta give this ta ya when you got older."

She opened the box to reveal an antique silver ring with a large diamond inset in silver leaves which wove themselves into a Celtic knot that made up the band. I blinked at it as she explained, "This was me mother's wedding ring, it was passed down ta me, then yer Ma, and now ta you."

She smiled toward the sittin' room where we could hear Lenore laughin' heartily at somethin' her siblings had said. It was such a wondrous sound to me.

I accepted the little box, and I tilted it in the bedroom's lamp light to see that light sparklin' along it like a livin' thing. Then I looked at Nana and shared a knowin' smile with her as I turned mahy gaze to the sitting room and said ta her, “I've just the thing ta do with it.” I started toward the door.

The End

Romance Novels by Erik Schubach

Books in the Music of the Soul universe...

(All books are standalone and can be read in any order)

Music of the Soul
A Deafening Whisper
Dating Game
Karaoke Queen
Silent Bob
Five Feet or Less
Broken Song
Syncopated Rhythm
Progeny
Girl Next Door
Lightning Strikes Twice
June
Dead Shot

Music of the Soul Shorts...

(All short stories are standalone and can be read in any order)

Misadventures of Victoria Davenport: Operation Matchmaker
Wallflower
Accidental Date
Holiday Morsels

Books in the London Harmony series...

(All books are standalone and can be read in any order)

Water Gypsy
Feel the Beat
Roctoberfest
Small Fry
Doghouse
Minuette
Squid Hugs
The Pike
Flotilla

Books in the Pike series...

(All books are standalone and can be read in any order)

Ships In The Night

Books in the Flotilla series...

(All books are standalone and can be read in any order)

Making Waves

Novels by Erik Schubach

Books in the Djinn series...
Cursed

Books in the Urban Fairytales series...
Red Hood: The Hunt
Snow: The White Crow
Ella: Cinders and Ash
Rose: Briar's Thorn
Let Down Your Hair
Hair of Gold: Just Right
The Hood of Locksley

Books in the Techromancy Scrolls series...
Adept
Soras
Masquerade (Winter 2016)
Outrider (Summer 2017)

Books in the Drakon series...
Awakening
Dragonfall

Books in the Valkyrie Chronicles series...
Return of the Asgard
Bloodlines
Folkvangr
Seventy Two Hours
Titans

Books in the Bridge series...
Trolls
Traitor
Unbroken

Books in the Fracture series...
Divergence

Books in the Paranormals series...
Fleas
This Sucks
Jinx (Winter 2016)

Short Stories by Erik Schubach
(These short stories span many different genres)

The Hollow
A Little Favor
Lost in the Woods
Rift Jumpers: Faster Than Light
Scythe
Snack Run
Something Pretty

Excerpt from Techromancy Scrolls: Masquerade...

Chapter 1 – Outrider

My foster daughter, Misty, came running into the study where I sat with Celeste and mother. She was blurting out, "Sora Laney, Sora Laney!" I gave her a chastising and expectant look. The girl smiled and gave us a far too cute embarrassed look as she rolled her eyes, correcting herself, "Sorry... mom."

I grinned like a loon as I leaned out of the sitting couch and gave the young one a hug and chuckled out as I ruffled her hair with my white silk gloved hand, "Better. Now what has you in such a tizzy?" Inside I was beaming with such warmth at her calling me that. I couldn't fault her, Celeste and I hadn't been her fosters for a month yet so it would take some time for us all to acclimate to our new family.

Celeste beamed at the two of us, she knows how happy I was was to take little Misty Cobbler in as a foster, once her gifts as a sensitive started getting more and more pronounced last year after she tuned nine. I admit to having a soft spot in my heart for all children and have had a deep yearning to have some of my own. Misty is the first of what I hope is many. And though she always tries to act aloof about it, she loves Misty dearly too.

I remember the tears of joy her parents had the day they accepted my offer of the fosterage of their daughter. It meant their child would live as a noble under the crest of my house and that she would want for nothing. That was a dream that was common among the serfs, I should know, it was a dream of mine once upon a time.

And unlike most fosterings, I buck the tradition of isolating the child from her birth parents by allowing them to visit her here, or for her to visit them any time she or they feel the urge. I think it is barbaric to not allow such.

My little brother, Jace, came darting into the study, bubbling with excitement, and his eager face fell when he saw Misty. He screwed up his face and narrowed one eye as he shook his head saying, "There is no way you could have beat me here you little sneak. I took every shortcut from the Warehouse District."

My brother had tuned into a strapping young man over the past three years since I returned from my adventures in Solomon. At twelve, he was taller and more fit than most of the kids his age, due to all of the running and hauling he did as the acknowledged fastest messenger in the court of Wexbury.

I am now able to finally envision what he will look like when he becomes an adult, now that he has lost most of the baby fat that children carry around the first ten years or so of their lives. His face was strikingly similar to my late step father, Corrick's. He is going to have girls following him around the court soon, which is just as well as he is starting to notice them.

Misty gave him her cute, disarming smile and said imperiously, "An aspiring Knight of the Realm must always take advantage of their environment to overcome any disadvantage." I had to grin at that and bite my tongue to stop the laugh that was threatening. She listened to Celeste's lessons more adamantly than I did myself, and was repeating it by rote.

Then she crinkled her nose and admitted through a grin, "I stowed away in a supply wagon returning to the castle from the warehouses, Uncle Jace."

Jace tipped his head back and laughed heartily. He was a good sport about being cheated from his victory. Then he shook his head and smiled at her as he pointed his finger accusingly at her, saying, "As I said, you're a little sneak." She stuck her tongue out at him. I was so glad that those two got along so well, especially since they were only three years apart and more like siblings than uncle and niece.

Celeste interjected, "Now that we have established the fact that our little Misty here is indeed and grade A sneak. What has the two of you so excited?"

Jace stood tall, turned his smile between the three of us adults, then just before he could speak, Misty blurted out, "The Junior Regiment has been tasked to inform you that Lord Bex says, 'It's time.'"

Jace blurted, "There is no such thing as the Junior Regiment. I was supposed to tell Laney, you were just sneaking around the area when you overheard him ask me."

My excitement was building. Our dear friend and fellow Knight, Sir Bexington, had been tinkering on a huge project for almost five years in the new warehouse he had commissioned in the warehouse district. He was so secretive about it and didn't even let his own wife, Lady Brenda in to see. Curiosity has been killing all the scholars and locals. His cobbled together mechanical technology failed more often than succeeded, but when he has one of his rare successes, the rest of the Lower Ten stands to take notice.

The gangly man has been hinting that he was almost ready to unveil his latest contraption, and it sounds like he is ready. I stood and separated the kids as Misty countered, "Yuh-ha, my Penny Lady put me in charge of the regiment, and she is a Sora so her word is law."

I ruffled both of their hair and said, "Are we going to belabor the point or are we going to see Bex's latest attempt at breaking his own fool neck?"

Celeste stood and said, "Shoo, get the horses, hitch the carriage for Lady Margret." She got a sheepish look on her face when mother cocked an eyebrow at her. My Lady amended, "I mean, for mother." The kids darted out, arguing over who got to hitch up the carriage. Then Celeste told mom, "It is just hard to get used to. I never thought I would marry, let alone to an impossible herder girl who will not yield." Mother just grinned and shrugged, her eyes glittering with joy, her eyebrow still cocked.

Celeste dropped her eyes like a chastised child and said through her little smirk, which did some interesting things to me, "Yes, ma'am." This got a chuckle from mom and a restrained one from me.

My betrothed grasped my hand, lacing our fingers and not caring about the missing finger under my glove. She didn't seem to see all my scars and flaws that made people stare as we walked by.

She shook my hand a bit and looked down, she always seemed to know when I wad feeling self doubt and she said softly, “I love you Laney.”

I blushed from my cheeks to the tips of my toes. I asked in earnest, “Really?”

She nodded and replied in everyone's ongoing joke about my height, “Just a little.”

I grinned up at her and said with longing in my voice as I looked at this Knight of the Realm who had chosen me over all the people clamoring for her attentions, “Good, because I love you too.”

We headed out of mother's manor, where we call home now. Until we can make Misty a squire in four years, she is not allowed to live in our quarters in the barracks. So we moved our little family into mother's manor just outside the castle gates. It had plenty of room with only mom and Jace living in it. Misty has her own room there, while Celeste and I sleep in the gypsy wagon which we were gifted by the Great Mother of the mountain gypsies herself, Ranelle.

Made in the USA
Lexington, KY
23 November 2017